Take Me

and other stories

Lisa Williams Kline

Lisa Williams Kline

MINT HILL BOOKS
MAIN STREET RAG PUBLISHING COMPANY
CHARLOTTE, NORTH CAROLINA

Cover artwork by: Kelsey Rebecca Kline

Acknowledgments:

The author gratefully acknowledges the editors of the publications who first published these stories:

An Intricate Weave: "Stage Fright"
The Belletrist Review: "Take Me"
Cicada: "This is for Janet"
Independence Boulevard: "Why I Hate Phone Solicitation"
Journey Without: 2009 Charlotte Writers' Club Anthology: "Guest Room"
Main Street Rag: "Groundrush"
Peregrine: "Webs"
Press 53: "Must Remain Anonymous"
Women's Words: "Take Me"

Library of Congress Control Number: 2010928968

ISBN: 978-159948-242-2

Produced in the United States of America

Mint Hill Books
Main Street Rag Publishing Company
PO Box 690100
Charlotte, NC 28227-7001
www.MainStreetRag.com

For Jeff

Contents

GROUNDRUSH

"…with invisible threads, a human life, and man who by stitches, cloth and cord, had made himself a god of the sky for those immortal moments…How tightly should one hold onto life? How loosely give it rein?"

—Charles A. Lindbergh,
on contemplating his first parachute jump

Billy and three other guys met every Saturday and jumped out of a Twin Otter that Teresa, who was thirty-four, was pretty sure was older than she was. One of the guys was an ex-con, one was a drop-out Marine, one was a rich, crazy college kid, and then there was Billy. Arty, who lived in a trailer next to the drop zone, flew the plane.

Teresa had been seeing Billy for less than two weeks when he first asked her to come watch him skydive. After a month, she gave in, and one Saturday they drove out to the drop zone outside Fayetteville in his dinged-up truck. The truck stalled on the dirt road on the way in, and the engine made a sick noise like the gnashing of metal teeth. It growled to life again when Billy smacked the dashboard and said "Down, boy, down."

"Dive with me, Teresa. Come on." Billy's wiry blonde hair was just long enough to pull back in a curled-up furry caterpillar of a ponytail. "We can go out tandem. I'll take care of you; you don't have to do a thing."

"I'll just wait for you over here," Teresa said. She headed for a picnic table not far from the wind sock. Billy said the guys liked to joke about the way the wind sock got a hard-on in the wind. "You boys jump til your hearts' content. I'm going to lay out in the sun. Come wake me up when you're done."

She spread a towel on top of the table and lay on her stomach with a magazine and smiled up at him.

"The guys at the drop zone have a motto," Billy said. "Boogie til you bounce."

"Til you bounce?" She squinted up at him. The sun was behind him and he seemed like an alien figure burned against the landscape.

"Yeah. Burn in. Buy the farm. Meet the Turk." He lit a cigarette, inhaled deeply, and balanced it on the edge of the picnic table. He unrolled his jumpsuit and stepped into it, pulling it over his shorts and t-shirt.

"You boys have so many cute little ways of saying a person's dead."

He silently buckled on his harness and pack.

He seemed annoyed, so Teresa asked, "Did you ever dive with anybody who...died?"

"Once. Guy just flipped over on his back so he wouldn't get groundrush and never pulled the ripcord."

"You mean he did it on purpose?"

"Yeah. He had a few problems."

"I guess."

He sat on the picnic table beside her, picked up his cigarette, dragged on it. "Boogie til you bounce. If you're gonna live, then, goddammit, live."

How juvenile he sounded, she thought. Yet, her skin quivered as he took his index finger and ran it gently down her backbone and underneath the waistband of her shorts.

"Quit it," she said. "I'm mad at you."

"You are not."

"Am too." Teresa sat up and slapped his hand.

"Come on, Teresa, I just want you to have a little fun. All you do is work in the produce department and fight with Sherry."

"I'm going to have lots of fun, thanks, laying in the sun on this picnic table with my magazine."

"When you're old and gray and dying, you'll say, shit, I never tried that."

"Believe it or not, I can live with it."

"If we did a tandem, we'd be strapped together, I'd take care of everything."

"If I killed myself jumping out of a plane, what would happen to Sherry?"

"You don't trust me, do you?"

She started to laugh, but then looked up at him and saw how earnest he looked. His eyebrows were knitted so that stray hairs at the center stood straight up. At the store Teresa listened without comment to her co-workers' pissant complaints about their husbands who left wet towels on the floor or tracked mud through the house. "Sherry's dad lives fifteen minutes from us," she said to Billy. "Sherry hasn't seen him in ten years. Since she was six."

"Can't you tell what we have is different?"

She smartly flipped a page of her magazine to conceal the dizzying rush of confusion she felt. So much did seem different about Billy. There was an energy about him that everyone wanted a piece of. He'd gotten to know almost everyone in her building in just a few weeks, people Teresa didn't even know herself, and once they found out he was an electrician they called him all the time now to take a look at something or other. Teresa didn't let him smoke in the apartment, because she was trying to quit, and sometimes he smoked and played cards with the widows in 3B, who took his money every time because he was a reckless, hopelessly optimistic card player and couldn't bluff for shit. But still. He was so young. "Why do you want me to jump out of airplanes? Why can't we just go dancing?"

Billy's brown eyes flickered, maybe with frustration, maybe with anger, and then he sighed. "We can go dancing if you want."

"You go on and jump. When we get home, I picked up a turkey breast on special. Then we could rent a movie. Unless that's too boring for you."

He lowered his blue goggles and trudged toward the plane. *That's not what I meant to say*, she wanted to shout after him. *What do you see in me?* She was doing everything wrong but she didn't know how to stop herself. She kept thinking there was no sense in trusting him, he would be gone any day.

But she never read her magazine at all. For twenty minutes she stared at the spot where she'd lost the buzzing plane in the clouds. When the plane emerged the divers dropped like tiny spiders in the wind. They tumbled over and over, airborne acrobats, then came together and grabbed hands and formed a flying circle, and a four-pronged star.

As they plummeted, she watched, squinting, her heart in her throat. Their chutes bubbled out, trailing by invisible threads, and bloomed into narrow rainbow-colored beehives. Billy had said it took seven hundred feet for a parachute to open. And then they began to glide, sometimes lazily, sometimes steering and soaring like birds.

By the time Arty landed the plane, the divers had hit their targets and gathered their arms full of the brilliant, slippery chutes.

"Fuckin' 'ey..!"

"What a rush!"

Their jubilant voices whipped by her in the wind as they carried their chutes back to the runway and laid them on the ground. Teresa watched how Billy rushed to fold his chute, so he wouldn't miss the next run. The college kid came over and, after dumping insults on Billy's chute-folding ability, precisely refolded his chute for him.

"So, what'd you think?" Billy looked streamlined, almost weightless, standing there in his jumpsuit. Teresa felt squat, like years of fighting gravity had started to flatten her against the earth.

"I'm not doing that."

"I'll make you change your mind," he said, grinning.

From the beginning Sherry gave Teresa a hard time about being older than Billy.

"Hey, Mom," she said one night, when Teresa had fixed barbecued ribs for the three of them, "did you realize that there's exactly the same number of years between me and Billy as there are between you and Billy?" She kind of slanted her eyes at Billy and licked barbecue sauce from the ends of her fingers. "I'm sixteen, Billy's twenty-five, you're thirty-four. Exactly nine years between each of us."

"Yeah, so?"

"I don't know. I was just saying." Sherry looked a lot like Teresa had at her age. Neither was pretty, since they had stringy brown hair and what Teresa's mother called "a DeGaulle nose" from her dad's side of the family, but they were both naturally thin, had good hipbones, and tanned well. So far there seemed to be nothing of Roger in Sherry, thank God, and Teresa would personally kill her if she ever took a drink.

"Can Wayne come over?" Sherry said.

"Don't you have homework?" Billy said, moving his knee against Teresa's under the table.

Sherry flounced out of the room.

Teresa got some face cream. Her hair was sprouting gray like crabgrass, so she was stopped in the hair care aisle, propping a box of radishes on her hip, when Fran and Linda from the bakery peeked around the corner. Fran had a tray of muffins and Linda carried an armload of French baguettes.

"Hey, Teresa, trying to look good for somebody?"

"When you rob the cradle it puts the pressure on, huh?"

"All right, all right." She held up two boxes. "Cocoa or espresso?"

"Cocoa is something you sip before bed. Espresso keeps you up." Linda winked at Fran, gesturing suggestively with a baguette. "You want to go to bed or stay up?"

"Why don't you ladies just shut the hell up," Teresa said. Linda and Fran laughed.

Teresa started doing sit-ups and leg lifts. Her plan was to make sure the light was off the first time she and Billy had sex in case the effect hadn't kicked in just yet.

Instead, the night after that first jump, he came up behind her in the kitchen and buckled his arms around her waist, pressing himself snug against her back. "This is how it would be if we jumped tandem," he said, the warm tickle of his mustache close to her ear. "We'd be strapped together and you'd be free-falling; I'd be right above you, whispering in your ear, just like this." He spread her arms like wings and leaned forward slightly and waltzed her around the den, making a *Shhhh-hhh-hhh* flying sound. "When you're way up high, you have this fairytale feeling of power, this amazing adrenalin rush, no words can describe it." He waltzed her from the living room into the hallway. "And the world down below looks tame and peaceful, the roads outlining the farms, houses in neat rows. Not a single wave in the water, just the edge of the water like lace." They skimmed like mating dragonflies into the bedroom. "And then, before you start feeling groundrush, you pull the ripcord. For a tandem that would be at five or six thousand feet. "

"What is groundrush, anyway? You talk about it all the time."

"When you get down to under a thousand feet the earth slams up to meet you. People say it's only when you get groundrush that you start to feel afraid."

Teresa turned around and put her hands on his chest to push him away, but he took her hands in his and kissed them. The blood pumped wildly in the tips of her fingers.

"I'd be totally in control of your ripcord," he said. "There would nothing for you to be scared of."

He peeled her T-shirt up and she raised her arms, letting him lift away the burden of years of her life. He was breathing into her hair now. They never did turn off the light. They fell asleep afterwards spread-eagle on the bed.

The second time they went to the drop zone Billy just about drove her crazy, nagging her to jump tandem with him. He finally managed to convince her to go up in the Otter just to watch. The seats had all been ripped out so they sat on the floor. The guys had on their gear and were adjusting the straps on their packs. Billy had even put a rig on Teresa because regulations required it. It made her nervous.

"Arty, go up to thirteen thousand," Billy said. "I want to punch through some clouds."

The plane buzzed like one of those fat lumbering bumblebees that you can't believe actually flies. Teresa was wedged against the back wall with Billy holding her hand. The wind through the door opening behind the wing was cold and deafening, and as they climbed her ears popped. Their voices grew higher, more excited, and the wind grew colder. The guys compared altimeters. Billy had forgotten his, of course.

"Hold onto this." His breath was close to her ear. "Don't let go." He wrapped her hand around a frayed handhold hanging from the ceiling and kissed her. His mustache and lips were both cold from the height and the wind. It was the coldest kiss Teresa had ever had. Then he put on his helmet.

"You guys ready?" shouted Arty from the cockpit.

They crouched facing her, their backs to the opening, chanting in unison.

"One potato, two potato, three potato, four...
five potato, six potato, out the fuckin' door!"

Billy grinned at her through his helmet and back flipped into the screaming white.

He shrank away with a whoosh, then disappeared into a cloud.

Hot bile raced up Teresa's throat.

"You OK?" Arty shouted.

She could barely nod.

She was at work on Monday and couldn't leave when the guidance counselor called to say Sherry wasn't in school. She begged her manager to take her lunch early, but he said he couldn't spare her. Desperate, she called Billy, who rearranged appointments and went over to the apartment and found Sherry in bed with Wayne.

When Teresa got home at four, Billy was sitting with Sherry at the kitchen table. Wayne had gotten his bony ass out of there. Teresa was too mad to talk to Sherry, to even look at her. How could she be so stupid? Hadn't she figured anything out? Teresa was conscious of the angry noise she made, stomping in, throwing her keys on the counter. Blood pumped next to her collarbone. She didn't even get within arm's reach of Sherry because she was afraid she'd shake her teeth out.

Sherry sighed with boredom, picked up a hunk of her dark hair and fanned it like a hand for cards, looking for split ends.

"I've been trying to tell Sherry what you do in high school may not seem so important but it is. When I was in high school I started running with the wrong people," Billy started out.

"The voice of experience." Sherry flicked her hair behind her ear and stared at the floor. They'd both heard Billy's stories about the months he was on probation several times.

"Listen, I just want to save you some of the shit I went through."

"You don't really care about me. You're just afraid if my mom has to spend too much time worrying about me she won't have time for you." Sherry pointedly took a long cigarette from her back pocket and put it between her lips. She let it hang there while she opened the book of matches. She wouldn't raise her eyes to meet Teresa's.

"That's not true," Billy said.

"Bullshit." Sherry jutted out her chin.

Billy yanked the cigarette out of her mouth and broke it.

"Billy!" Teresa said it before she could think. "This is between me and her; it has nothing to do with you." Her voice became softer as she realized what she had said, and sank to almost nothing at the end.

Billy looked shocked. He stood up, and held his hands out the way men do sometimes to say *I'm not touching this.* He grabbed his jean jacket from the back of the chair and left.

Billy didn't call her after that. The first few days she didn't even notice. She was running back and forth to the school, meeting with the guidance counselor and teachers. They told her it wasn't the first time Sherry had skipped. She was failing two classes and wouldn't graduate in the spring unless she brought the grades up. Teresa finally managed to arrange with her store manager to work morning hours so she could be home in the afternoons.

"Jesus, Mom." One night, after they finally started speaking, Sherry lay on the couch and plopped her feet in Teresa's lap for her to rub them the way she always did. Sherry scrutinized her split ends. "We're not chained together."

"Wanna bet?" Teresa shot back, wanting to chop off every damn strand of Sherry's hair. "Yes we are, Sherry, we're stuck with each other forever."

Sherry dropped the hank of hair and interrupted softly. "And you hate me right?"

Teresa's anger rushed away, and, with her fingertips, she traced the strong bones of Sherry's ankles, feeling a link to her daughter so strong that it was hard to tell where one of them ended and the other began. "I love you more than anything. I don't want life to be hard for you, that's all."

One Friday night Teresa was watching TV with Sherry when one of the widows from 3B called to see if Billy could look at their fuse box.

"He's not here," Teresa said. She started to offer to call him, but realized she was too proud to call first. "Try him at home. I'll give you his number."

'Oh," said the widow. "All right. Well, if you and Sherry aren't busy you're welcome to join us for a little blackjack. It's only nickel ante."

"No thanks," she said. "I don't gamble." She felt sorry the minute she said it. Billy used to tell her she had a bad attitude. No matter what happened, he said, Teresa always looked at the negative side of things. That was OK, though, he said, since he always looked at the positive side. They were perfect for each other, according to Billy, because positive and negative together make electricity.

That was when she started trying to call him. She hit the redial key over and over, just like she used to do for radio contests in high school. It was like this thunderbolt hit her right between the eyes.

He didn't answer until ten-thirty.

"Hi. Been at the drop zone?"

"Hey, Teresa." Billy's voice was surprised, cautious. "Yeah, just got back."

"Listen, I hadn't heard from you. You OK?"

"Yeah. Fine."

"Hey, I got some turkey breast on sale. Just kidding. You want to come over?" she said.

"How about you come over to my place?"

She glanced at Sherry, who was watching under her starched bangs, waiting for what she was going to say to Billy on the phone. Wouldn't she love to be left alone for a few hours.

"I can't leave Sherry by herself," she said. "She's grounded."

A few seconds of silence on the other end of the phone. Sherry stalked out of the room.

"OK," Billy said. "Be there in a couple minutes."

Teresa cracked open the front door, breathed in the reckless shimmer of the summer night through the screen, then frantically looked for her new jeans. They were wadded on the floor of Sherry's closet. "Sherry, I swear, how many times do I have to tell you to quit trashing my clothes?"

"Relax, Mom. Wear my black ones. They'll be sexier anyway."

"That's not the point." Teresa hopped on one foot, pulling on the black jeans. "Where the hell's my mascara?" She was extra careful putting on her make-up. She'd almost ruined it. She didn't plan to screw up again.

Her mouth was full of toothpaste and she thought about his mustache and the aura of energy that just seemed to hover around him while the widow's nasty little dog started to bark and brakes screeched down in the intersection and she was thinking that maybe she would just jump tandem with him, she'd let him talk her into it, why the hell not? and a minute later, as the curling iron sizzled her bangs, far in the distance she heard sirens, then close by the two widows from 3B coming down the breezeway, passing her open door, talking.

"Hazel, I just realized, this is the same thing I wore to the last accident."

She didn't even look out, just kept putting on her make-up, thinking that Sherry was playing Coldplay way too loud and she started to yell at her to turn it down, but then she remembered that Billy especially liked this song, "Fix Me," so she didn't. And then, five minutes later, one of the widows banged on her door, screaming "Teresa!"

As she raced down the hill to the intersection a cop grabbed her arm. "You don't want to go down there," he said.

The morning after, Teresa picked up Billy's black comb and cigarettes from the intersection. Believe it or not, the half pack of Winstons he carried in his shirt pocket was only slightly crushed. On the asphalt was a spray paint outline of his body, arms straight out and legs slightly spread, just the way it looked in free fall.

Sometimes in sci-fi movies people have this green glow around them for a few seconds after the aliens zap them. And then they disappear without a trace. Or sometimes they leave inanimate objects, like combs and cigarettes, which only minutes ago seemed to breathe with their very own life.

Day after day over the following week Teresa replayed in her mind how far his body had flown, how hard it must have hit the pavement. Her entire body hurt, as though she'd been beaten. She ached and shivered like she had the flu. She cried at unexpected times, while restocking lettuce or mopping the floor. And still, after seven days, down in the intersection, that spray-paint outline of his body was still there. Teresa had to look at it every day on the way to and from work. She was seeing that green outline in her dreams. One day she called the police. "Listen, can't somebody get rid of it?"

The desk sergeant said that she sympathized but that the outline was necessary for the insurance companies involved and the elements would take care of it in due time.

"So what you're telling me," Teresa shouted, "is that I have to wait for it to rain?"

Lisa Williams Kline

His mother called when she came to town to get his body. "He told me about you," she said. Teresa couldn't believe it. He had? His mother planned to take him back to Raleigh for the funeral, and invited Teresa to come.

"That's so nice of you to ask," Teresa said, knowing she wouldn't go. But they talked for awhile and Teresa liked the breathy, headlong way his mother talked, just like Billy.

Teresa used to sleep like a baby lying next to him and didn't even appreciate the luxury of it. Now she couldn't sleep at all. Sherry cried a lot and said how sorry she was and signed up for summer school and even broke up with Wayne, but Teresa still couldn't sleep. One night about four Teresa put on some jeans and a sweatshirt and got a can of turpentine, some scrub brushes and a bucket of hot water.

She walked down to the intersection, and there was Billy in freefall, under the garish cycling stoplight, all she had left of him. She remembered him standing in the sunshine at the drop zone with his parachute in his arms. That jumpsuit made him look like he was from some futuristic starship, maybe another planet. She could still feel the ice-cold kiss in the Twin Otter before he jumped.

"Mom, need some help?" Sherry had her hair in a ponytail, the way she wore it to bed, with her nightgown tucked into her jeans.

"Sure. Keep us alive." Teresa got down on her knees and scrubbed while Sherry waved cars around her. By dawn they had to stop because of traffic. The outline was dimmer but it hadn't gone away.

Afterwards she and Sherry sat at the kitchen table, drank coffee, and smoked Billy's last two Winstons. They swore they'd both quit again as soon as these were gone.

In the dizzying rush of her first nicotine in months, Teresa blew smoke in the air between them and tried to will Billy to materialize in the gray cloud, with his fuzzy little ponytail, like a genie. She wiped her wet cheeks, and looked out the window at a sliver of light behind the trees. "Oh, Sherry, I wish I'd jumped."

"You still could, Mom." Sherry's eyes, older than her sixteen years, narrowed against the smoke. "You still could."

STAGE FRIGHT

"Stage lights wash you out. You must have color, lots of color!" says Miss Floretta. "Shut your eyes."

Isabel watches as her daughter Anna closes her eyes and turns her face up for the dance teacher. Miss Floretta cakes blue eye shadow on the child's eyelids with bold rough strokes and smears rouge like red lollipops on Anna's six-year-old cheeks. Then she produces a lipstick in an electric shade of red and traces Anna's lips. Anna looks shockingly mature and Isabel winces.

"Now you." Miss Floretta takes hold of Isabel's chin. Isabel notices that Miss Floretta's helmet of red hair blazes even backstage. She wears an evening gown with flowing sleeves like the wings of a luna moth. Isabel shuts her eyes and feels the pricking of the make-up brushes on her eyelids and cheeks, then the waxy pressure of the lipstick.

"There." Miss Floretta squints, licks her finger, and rubs hard at a spot next to Isabel's eye. "Remember to smile. You're having the time of your life," she says grimly, over her shoulder, as she sails forward to grasp another chin.

Isabel reaches to smooth a stray blonde hair from Anna's forehead.

"Leave me alone." Anna jerks away.

For a moment, though, their faces are close and Isabel smells Anna's warm breath, which is still sweet and baby-like, still makes her almost faint with love and fear.

The fear reminds her with a shock about what happened to Leah McCurdy only two weeks ago, and her throat constricts. Some of the other mothers didn't even think it was appropriate for them to go forward with the recital. But Miss Floretta insisted. "The show must go on," she said. They re-choreographed the dance, without Leah and her grandmother, whom Isabel had so admired for being out there hoofing it at sixty-eight. Leah's grandmother tapped with serenity and economy of motion, as if she could dance with a tea set balanced on her head. As if, in water, she would create barely a ripple. Isabel sent a note and flowers. She did not go to the funeral and did not tell Anna.

No one had known where Leah's mother was. Someone said they thought Leah's mother had disappeared and left Leah with the grandmother several years before. But nobody had ever asked the grandmother about it. For an hour each week they just danced, as if this was an island in their lives, and nothing else mattered except learning the combinations. Isabel had liked that. She thought Anna had too.

Two girls wearing hot pink sequins, a year or two older than Anna, are chanting a playground nonsense rhyme with clapping and hand motions to go with it. *"Money back too green, I want a jelly bean. Jelly bean not yummy, I want to see your tummy."*

"Let's practice," Anna says, pulling Isabel's hand. Isabel is left-handed (thus left-footed) and her inclination is to do most dance steps backwards.

"No, Mommy, other foot. Watch me again."

Anna is a natural. She memorizes combinations with ease, while Isabel, having recently crammed her brain with new job responsibilities and childcare arrangements, can't remember what comes after shuffle-hop-step to save her life. Practicing dance steps with Anna has been an exercise in humiliation so complete Isabel would have quit except the family therapist had said this joint mother-daughter activity was good for Anna.

"If Miss Shelton doesn't come I'll kill myself," Anna says, as they finish the run-through.

"No, you won't, don't be silly."

Miss Shelton, during the parent-teacher conference in November, described Anna as an underachiever who misbehaves to get attention. Anna is in love with Miss Shelton's shirtwaist dresses and round, perfect vowels and has no idea Miss Shelton might not love her back.

Now Anna peeks through the black velvet curtain, although Miss Floretta has told everyone not to, red feathers bobbing both on her head and from the curve of her bottom."Mommy, there are so many people out there!" She makes a face of mock terror. But Isabel knows Anna is looking forward to being onstage and having people watch her.

With Isabel the terror is real. Her throat muscles and kneecaps are shaking. She remembers a home movie of herself at five, dressed in a pink tutu, with a blonde ponytail like Anna's, standing on the front sidewalk of their brick house. In the silent film, her mother, dressed in a Jackie Kennedy style pastel sheath dress with white gloves, asks her to do something, and Isabel shakes her head. Even in black and white, her face is ashen.

Whenever her family watches this home movie, her father, in shadow behind the projector, says, "Remember, sweetie? You wouldn't do a dance step for the camera."

Her mother, curled next to Isabel on the couch, rubs Isabel's arm and says, "You ended up not dancing in the recital. The teacher couldn't get you to go onstage. But you were so darling."

And Isabel always says, "Those talent scouts from American Ballet Theatre must've been just devastated." But she always notes the way the tights bag around her ankles, the way the tulle on her skirt droops and she hates her five-year-old self.

"I see Granma and Granpa." Anna pokes her head and arm through the curtain and waves.

"Get your arm back in here this minute, young lady!" Miss Floretta yanks the curtain shut. "It is highly unprofessional, highly unprofessional, to wave at the audience. You spoil the grand illusion." She guides Anna away by her shoulders.

Miss Floretta Garland came from textile money, made somewhat of a name for herself playing Cassie in "A Chorus Line" on Broadway, returned fifteen years later and turned the downstairs of the white-columned family mansion into a dance studio. She lives alone upstairs, a husband having left her decades ago. She has one son who, after twenty years of pliés, moved to North Dakota and works on a dude ranch. Another mom told Isabel that every year, on recital weekend, he sends a basket of Harry and David's fruit, but has never returned.

"I didn't see Daddy," Anna says over the staccato clicking of tap shoes and taut pre-show chatter.

Isabel is half-furious Charles might have forgotten his daughter's recital, half-relieved he may miss seeing Isabel make a fool out of herself. He has seen the pink tutu home movie more than once. She is sure Charles' new girlfriend danced at every recital and probably did a solo as well. Isabel pictures Marcia smiling and curtseying as roses of all colors land on stage at her feet.

"I'm sure he's here," she says. "He wouldn't miss seeing you dance."

"What about Dwayne? Is he coming too?" Anna steals another peek through the curtain.

"Maybe. Remember, Miss Floretta said not to look at the audience." Isabel has discouraged Dwayne from coming. She believes any possibilities there might be in their relationship could be compromised by her basic resemblance, while onstage, to an ostrich.

But Anna has already seen Dwayne making his way down the center aisle, so anxious to prove his devotion to both Isabel and Anna he's brought two bouquets the size of azalea bushes. He looks like the FTD man. He spots Isabel's parents and holds the flowers above his head as he edges past several pairs of knees and sits right behind them. Carefully laying the flowers in his lap, he reaches over the back of a chair to shake hands with Isabel's father.

He looks up, sees Anna and Isabel, both peeking from behind the curtain, and blows them a kiss. Isabel feebly moves her fingers up and down in acknowledgement.

"Dwayne is a dork," Anna says.

Dwayne does research with fruit flies. Isabel noticed one floating out of Dwayne's hair the first time they kissed. On his desk he keeps dead fruit flies in a jar of formaldehyde labeled "Ashes to Ashes, Dust to Dust."

"Shoo, shoo, shoo!" Miss Floretta waves them away from the wings as the lights dim and the first trumpeting strains to "One," from "Chorus Line," which is Miss Floretta's theme song, blare from the backstage sound system.

Anna takes Isabel's hand as they all file downstairs to the musty-smelling dressing room under the stage to wait for their cues. Isabel's hand is cold, Anna's is warm. The saxophones and trumpets slide down the scales and up again as "One" draws to a close. Tiny flying flecks of feather boas of all colors—pink, yellow, red, blue, and white—float to the gray scratched linoleum and slide like sailboats. Sequins and tiaras sparkle. The air snaps with nervous energy.

"Good evening." Miss Floretta's voice comes from above, muffled as it seeps through the floorboards. There is supposed to be a sound system down here so the dancers can hear when they have to go on, but it never works, so over the years they have developed a method of taking turns climbing from a chair to the radiator and holding a tall glass up to the ceiling and placing an ear next to it. Now a teenager in white fringe stands on top of the radiator and translates, stopping every few seconds to listen.

"As always...I am delighted to present my students in this year's recital...I would like to dedicate tonight's performance to Leah McCurdy. All profits from ticket sales...will go to a fund for battered children."

"Why is she dedicating the recital to Leah?" Anna pokes Isabel. "You told me Leah moved to Myrtle Beach with her mother. You said she could go swimming every day."

Isabel pretends she doesn't hear. How do you tell a child something like that? Last week one of the other mothers called and told Isabel that the counselor from Leah's school had offered to have a special meeting with the girls Leah danced with to talk about what had happened. Isabel said no thanks. What help would it do to talk?

Anna already has trouble sleeping. Since Charles moved out, she helps Isabel check and recheck the window locks every night. Often she climbs in bed with Isabel. Sometimes Isabel climbs in bed with her. Then Isabel holds her and strokes the silky blonde hairs on her arms. At first she used to ask, "Mommy, are you crying?" but now she doesn't any more, and Isabel almost feels they are going to get through this.

"Leah got killed from her stepfather hitting her," says a girl in blue sequins with a shiny black ponytail.

Anna stares at the other child, her lipsticked mouth open.

The applause ends. The first song of the recital begins. The dancers in the second number, dressed in puffs of yellow like chicks, are lined up by one of Miss Floretta's assistants and escorted upstairs. One of the chicks has a slick red face and is sobbing.

"I don't believe you," Anna says.

"Yes, she did."

"Did not."

"Did too."

"Mom, did she?"

"Did she what?" Isabel stalls. She can't look at Anna's stricken face.

"Get killed from her stepfather hitting her?"

Isabel considers whether to lie or tell the truth, with only fifteen minutes before they are to go onstage, dance, and smile. She glares at the girl in blue, at the same time knowing it's not the child's fault. Who told that child what happened? What kind of parent would do such a thing?

Maybe Isabel should have told Anna. Maybe she should have taken her to the session with the counselor.

Isabel feels sick. Is it such a crime to want to protect your children from the world? Her mother has often asked, "Isabel, why must you cart that child everywhere? She's perfectly capable of riding her bike over to her friends' houses. You did! They're right in the neighborhood, for Pete's sake!" Isabel wants to tell her mother, but doesn't, that the principal sent a notice home just last week about a man in a gray car cruising the neighborhood, trying to get children to go for a ride with him.

Now she takes Anna's hand in both of hers.

"I promise we'll talk about it later, sweetie."

Anna suddenly punches Isabel's thigh. "I want to talk about it now! Did Leah get killed?"

"Yes," Isabel says at last. There is ringing in her ears. "It was a terrible, terrible thing that happened." Isabel glances at Anna's face, but can't hold Anna's eyes. She sees a run, like a ladder, in Anna's tights. "You have a run. I think I brought some nail polish. Hold still."

Isabel fishes through her purse, watching Anna's face. It has gone blank. She finds the clear nail polish and paints it, cool and thick, just above Anna's knee.

The girls in pink chant, *"Ooh, ahh, I want a piece of pie. Pie too sweet, I want a piece of meat. Meat not cooked, I want to read a book."*

"I didn't tell you," Isabel says, "because I was afraid of how upset you'd be. We'll talk about it after the recital, OK? There's even a lady at Leah's school who can talk to you about it. I'll call her tomorrow."

Isabel blows gently on the nail polish to dry it. Anna wipes the back of her hand across her face, smearing her eye shadow and lipstick.

"I feel bad because I didn't really like Leah that much."

"That's OK."

"One time I saw her steal a piece of gum from somebody else's backpack. She said she'd kill me if I told."

Isabel strokes the back of Anna's hand. She remembers Leah's narrow blue eyes, the serious angles of her cheeks, the willow-like brown hair. The hollows behind her collarbone and the slightly turned-in knobs of her knees. Leah's grandmother let her do whatever she liked. She'd shake her head, almost proud, and say, "I can't do a thing with her." She'd measured her words carefully, like spoonfuls of flour, when she told the other dancers that Leah's mother had gotten her act together and wanted Leah back. The mother wanted to take Leah to Myrtle Beach, and the plan was to bring her back for the weekend of the recital.

Now Isabel searches Anna's face, tries to read her thoughts through the blue-green windows of her eyes, and understand the conclusions she might be reaching.

"Is that why Leah's stepfather hit her? Because she was bad sometimes?"

"No! She wasn't bad."

"But you said not to take things from other people. She stole gum. That's bad."

"Sweetie, no, that's not it. Her stepfather was bad. Not Leah."

Anna is silent. She pushes herself into the corner, pulls her knees to her chin.

And the girls in pink chant, *"Bed not made, I want some lemonade. Lemonade too sour, I want to take a shower. Shower too wet, I want to get a pet.*"

Isabel sits next to Anna, stroking her hand.

"I don't want to do the dance," Anna finally says. "I want to go home."

"Let's try not to think about it. This is such a special night. Let's have a nice time dancing together, OK?" Isabel feels ridiculous saying these words. She doesn't want to dance either and wishes she could be in the dark cozy comfort of her parents' family room, watching the flickering black and white images of herself as a child, knowing that even though she didn't dance, she was still loved.

Another child from the mother-daughter routine climbs down from the radiator. Her tap shoes clatter on the floor. "We're next," she says.

Knees pop and costumes rustle as the mothers and daughters stand and begin to line up. The mothers preen their daughters with deft, thoughtless motions, as if they are not separate people, but simply extensions of themselves. Some daughters stand patiently, and others wiggle away. Some grip their mothers' arms or legs. One says her stomach hurts. The mothers' voices are high, taut, like violin strings in need of tuning. Finally they file out in a flurry of red boa and sequins. A few look at Isabel and Anna questioningly and say "Coming?" Isabel stands, slowly, but Anna remains in the corner.

"How do you know if someone is bad?"

Isabel hesitates, then slides down the wall and sits beside Anna, takes her hand. "You don't. It's very hard. But that's what I'm here for. To help you figure that out."

"You can tell?"

"Not always. It can be confusing because most people are not all bad and not all good, but some of both. But I promise I'll help you the best I can. OK?"

Anna is silent for a minute, considering what Isabel has said. Then, "Leah's grandmother is very sad, isn't she?"

"Yes. She loved Leah very much."

"We should go visit her and cheer her up."

Isabel wants to cry.

"OK. We will." She isn't surprised, really, that Anna has more courage than she does. She makes a promise to herself, that they really will go visit Leah's grandmother next week.

Miss Floretta appears in the doorway, her sleeves flapping like a flag on the battlefield.

"There you are! Get your butts onstage *now*, ladies!"

She disappears.

Isabel stands and holds her hand out for Anna. Anna looks up at her, then reaches out. Isabel pulls her to her feet.

"Mommy, wait." Anna stands on tiptoe and gently plucks a wisp of red feather boa from one of Isabel's eyelashes.

Then, hand in hand, they run upstairs, blindly fight the heavy black stage curtains, and find their positions. As the first notes of "Yessir, That's my Baby" begin, Isabel sees Miss Floretta glaring at them like a Valkyrie. Isabel doesn't mind; she instead admires the straightness of Miss Floretta's back. She realizes Anna is gripping her hand, squeezing the blood out of her fingers. She pries her hand free, and whispers, "You're going to be great!" Then she pushes Anna out under the hot lights, and follows her.

In the blurry darkness just beyond the glare she sees her father's face riveted on the stage with a child-like expression of pride and delight. Her mother waves at Anna, in spite of several pre-show requests from both Isabel and Anna to refrain. Just behind them, Dwayne watches, his glasses glinting in the dark, grinning and cradling the two bouquets like twin babies. Isabel doesn't see Charles at all. She notices Miss Shelton in the second row.

She, for a moment, imagines Leah and her loose-skinned, light-hearted grandmother in their red sequins, tapping with the rest of them. She can almost see their faces.

She sees that Anna is beaming, performing, absorbing the audience's energy like a sponge. She sees from the tilt of Anna's head, the way the moves her shoulders, the shimmering aura around her, that whatever "it" is, Anna's got it.

Isabel has already made a couple of mistakes, but she hasn't fallen, and she has decided if she does, what the hell, she will just get up and keep dancing.

"Smile!" Miss Floretta shouts from the wings.

Isabel smiles.

TAKE ME

Laura tried to encourage independence in her kids in the event she should be abducted by aliens. Bob, addicted to his work as he was, would barely notice her absence, but she did worry about the kids. She hoped, if she were abducted, it would not be the night before a spelling test. Tuesday and Wednesday were her best times. At the same time, she realized that the kids were growing older each day, making their own sandwiches, putting on their own Band-Aids, and soon they wouldn't need her at all.

She read everything she could find about the abductions. People said they were lifted from their beds and floated, right through walls, up to the waiting spaceship. Then there seemed to be some kind of time warp. People stayed long enough to receive thorough examinations and for some women actually to be impregnated with mixed-breed embryos and give birth to them. But when they arrived back home they had been gone for only two days.

Laura did not believe the discomforts of the examinations people had described could be any worse than a regular check-up with her ob-gyn. She sometimes wondered how it would feel to be a mother to a half-human, half-alien embryo, to see it growing, to know it was the last best hope for a dying civilization. Fulfilling this desperate need was a comforting thought to her. She imagined bringing a snapshot back to the kids and saying, "Look, there's your baby sister."

One woman, who had experienced numerous abductions between the ages of four and twenty-something, described meeting her two half-alien daughters, wispy blonde creatures who hugged her shyly and said, "Mama, I love you." The *National Inquirer* had an artist's rendering of what the daughters looked like.

Just imagine! Laura Floyd, who had spent her lifetime, it seemed, folding clothes, packing lunches, and being polite to phone solicitors, could become mother to a savior of civilization. Not unlike the Virgin Mary. Why, it tended to blow one's mind.

Laura told no one of this. Not a soul. She wrote a note to the children and put it in an envelope labeled, "In the Event of My Disappearance." The note contained instructions on how to run their twelve-year-old washing machine and where she kept the appliance light bulbs for the refrigerator. Her pen poised above the paper, she felt, vaguely, there was something else of importance she should relate to the children, and to Bob, but couldn't think what it was, and quickly signed the note. She cut out a comprehensive article on extraterrestrial abductions, and put that and the letter in an envelope in her jewelry box.

She began to think of her nightgowns not just as sleepwear, but travel wear as well. She avoided filmy, see-through styles and tried to think in practical terms such as warmth, protection from rain, and so on. L.L. Bean was a good source.

Laura got into the habit of watching the skies at night. At first she had been unhappy with Bob's desire to live so far out in the country, away from neighbors, with such a long train ride to his office in Chicago. He left at five o'clock in the morning and returned sometimes as late as ten at night. He traveled often for weeks at a time.

But the sky was big here and the stars were brilliant. They spread over her each night, cool and comforting, as she lay on her back on a blanket in the yard. After the children were asleep she watched for spaceships and mentally beckoned the aliens. Aliens, she reasoned, could intercept her thoughts as she sent them whirling into the chill night air. Unlike Bob who, whenever Laura got upset, sputtered, "You can't expect me to read your mind!"

So each night she lay on her blanket, trembling a little, her senses on edge, waiting for something to happen. Sometimes she caught herself thinking about what it would be like to have sex with an alien. They had been described as small and hairless, with thin, unsensuous mouths but gentle, inquisitive eyes. She imagined she might be squeamish at first, but that the alien would possess certain mind-control capabilities which could drive her to paroxysms of ecstasy.

But she never saw anything. She heard an occasional owl, she saw airplanes and shooting stars. She often fell asleep out there and later wandered upstairs to her bed with dew in her hair.

One night she climbed into her empty bed, slept briefly, and when she swam up toward consciousness a few minutes later there was a man in bed beside her. She shrank away with a gasp. His rounded shoulder was just inches away. Then she noticed a bald spot at the crown of his head. She realized, feeling foolish, that the person was Bob, back early from a business trip.

But was the bald spot larger than she remembered? She studied the back of the head for long seconds. Was it Bob? At that moment the man groaned and turned onto his back, throwing his hand across his forehead with a sigh, giving her a full view of his profile. It did indeed look like Bob,

　　　　　　　　　　　　Lisa Williams Kline

though she couldn't remember studying his profile in this much detail ever before, and his mouth seemed less full than she remembered. There was a small red mole next to his ear that Laura did not remember at all.

Laura slipped out of bed and went in the bathroom, closing the door very slowly so it wouldn't squeak. She turned on the light and stared at herself in the mirror. A pale, thin face with large eyes looked back at her. Her curly dark hair was graying and badly cut. Her collarbone protruded from the neckline of her sensible, all-terrain nightgown. Yet her features seemed to be absolutely her own—not slightly altered, like Bob's.

What if the man lying beside her wasn't Bob, but an alien taking his place? Presumably his appearance could be approximated but, just as when you know one twin and look at the other, there would be slight inevitable differences. Her heart thumped hard, once. She decided to go back into the bedroom and study his profile again.

She turned off the light and soundlessly opened the door, then tiptoed toward the bed in the dark, waiting for her eyes to adjust. At that moment a thick, almost palpable beam of light shot through the window and traversed the room. The white sheets on her side of the bed, empty, almost blinded her. Then Bob's sleeping form was garishly illuminated in bluish yellow for a full two or three seconds, long enough for Laura to see a small hole in his T-shirt under the arm, a string hanging from his boxer shorts, and, on the hand flung in unconscious melodrama across his forehead, his too-tight wedding ring.

The beam of light lifted Bob from the bed and he hung suspended for a few seconds like a marionette. Then he was pulled suddenly and soundlessly through the window at incredible speed, his form shrinking in seconds to the size of an acorn.

The light disappeared and Laura stood in the blackness. She stumbled to the window, tried to look out, but the brilliance of the beam of light was still imprinted on her retinas. She blinked and passed her hand across her eyes.

When she looked out again, she saw only the stars and the lacy black tops of trees. An owl cried, "Who?"

Laura turned and looked at the empty bed. She was still so frightened she could feel her eyelids and kneecaps twitching, yet a hot flush of anger gathered in her throat. They had taken Bob instead of her!

The next day Laura punched pillows with a fury she had never before possessed. She broke dishes while jamming them into the dishwasher. Clothes ripped as she yanked them from the washing machine.

Men got to go everywhere and do everything. It just wasn't fair.

She shouted at the children to do their homework by themselves, how would they ever learn to be on their own if their mother did everything for them? She left their beds unmade and did not bother to pick their clothes off the floor.

She found an old pair of Bob's glasses under the bathroom sink and maliciously broke the earpieces off. How cruelly unfair, how patently unfair, that the aliens should take Bob instead of her.

She was sure by now it was all a mistake. The aliens had received her mental messages and come for her, and they'd taken Bob only because she happened not to be in bed at that moment. She replayed the events many times in her mind, each time chastising herself for getting up to go to the bathroom at just that instant.

As her anger cooled she decided that at any time Bob would be tossed from the lower atmosphere into the front yard, discarded, as it were, by the aliens, once they realized their mistake. It shouldn't take them long. After all, they had come for Laura, who had the utmost respect for them and their work, who was ready and willing to fulfill her destined role in the evolution of the universe—but they ended up with Bob, cynical, overweight, workaholic Bob. Imagine their disappointment!

The children, of course, did not question Bob's absence, since he was away so often. Laura continued her activities as usual, occasionally peeking out the window and scanning the front yard for Bob's prostrate form. That afternoon Richard, from Bob's office, called and asked for him.

"Uh, he got in late last night from his trip and is very sick," Laura said.

"We were wondering why we hadn't heard from him. He usually calls in five times a day."

It occurred to Laura that he had never called *her* five times a day, even in their first flush of sex together. Once, a few weeks ago, he'd called twice in an hour—once to say he missed the 5:37 and would try to catch the 6:12, then again to say he missed the 6:12 but would almost certainly, barring a catastrophe, be on the 6:37. As it turned out, he caught the 7:12.

"He probably won't be in tomorrow, either," she said to Richard now.

"Is he too sick to talk?" Richard asked. "We just have a couple of questions about an account."

"I'm afraid he's asleep right now."

Richard said he would try back the next day.

Laura decided that when Bob got back she would tell him in no uncertain terms exactly how she felt about his usurping her experience. At the same time she began to feel very excited about his return, making a mental list of questions to ask him. Could you exchange thoughts with the aliens? What color were their eyes? How did an alien's skin feel when you touched it?

When she awoke on the morning of the second day, a limp form lay beside her in the bed. Holding her breath, Laura pulled back the sheet. Bob's breathing was so shallow it was hard to tell if he was unconscious or just asleep. There were small puncture marks at his wrists and elbows, and on both his shorts and T-shirt there were a few very tiny dots of blood. He had two-days' beard stubble and one of his glasses lenses was missing. He smelled of stale sweat and antiseptic. Other than that, he appeared no different from when he left.

Should she call the rescue squad? She couldn't decide. She was sure no one would believe her story about the beam of light. Bob didn't have any life-threatening injuries that she could see. She decided not to call anyone just yet, got a washcloth, and began to wipe away the small dots of blood.

For the next few days, Bob floated in and out of consciousness. He didn't speak and his eyes, when he looked at her, showed no recognition. Laura got him to drink a little water but couldn't get him to eat, and he seemed to be losing weight before her eyes.

On the afternoon of his second day back, as she was very gently shaving the still sleeping Bob, it occurred to her that this physical caretaking was the closest thing to intimacy she'd had with her husband in a long time. She wiped the shaving cream from his face with a soft cloth, then stroked his now-smooth jaw with the backs of her fingers. Smooth-shaven and slimmer, with his face muscles relaxed in sleep, he reminded her of the young man she had married twelve years ago.

She told the children that their father was back from his business trip, but was very sick. Richard called several more times, and each time she said she simply couldn't bother Bob with work-related problems just yet.

Preoccupied with taking care of Bob, Laura forgot to take her blanket out into the yard to watch the sky. Instead, she sat in a chair beside Bob's bed, waiting for him to wake up. He seemed to have fitful dreams, mumbling to himself sometimes. Once she thought she heard him say, "How

Lisa Williams Kline

much do you want? I'll pay you ten thousand dollars. Just take me back."

How pitiful that Bob thought aliens would attach any value whatsoever to American money! Laura imagined several aliens, dressed in white coats, standing over Bob, laughing at this offer. How would an alien laugh, she wondered? Certainly not a guffaw, more, she imagined, a snicker, like Snoopy on the animated cartoon. She imagined Bob patting his boxer shorts, where his pockets should be, for his checkbook, saying, "Can you get me access to a FAX machine? A telephone? E-mail? And who should I have the check made out to?"

Around sundown of his third night home, Bob woke up. As Laura watched him focus on the familiar nubbed white bedspread, the pictures of the kids on the wall of their bedroom, and finally Laura's wedding portrait, she saw his bloodshot eyes fill, overflow. When his eyes rested on Laura sitting in the chair, she thought, my God, he has never really looked at me with love until this moment.

"Laura." His voice was a croak. He fumbled on the night stand for his glasses, examined where Laura had taped the earpieces, put them on.

"A lens was missing from your other ones," she said quickly. His eyes drank her in with such gratitude that she felt self-conscious, almost naked.

"The kids?" he asked.

"Spending the night with friends. They'll be back tomorrow."

He nodded.

"I saw the beam of light," she said. "Don't be afraid I won't believe you, because I know where you went."

"You do?" Incredulous for a moment, he then seemed to forget what he was thinking about. He rubbed his hand across his cheek. "Did you shave me?"

She nodded.

"Funny," he said then. "I remembered every detail of where I was until just a minute ago. It sort of slipped away."

"The beam of light," Laura prompted.

Bob looked at her blankly.

"The spaceship?"

He blinked.

Laura's disappointment was so acute tears burned her eyes. First Bob got to go instead of her, and now he couldn't even tell her what it was like. She clenched her fists and took a deep, ragged breath.

Then she remembered reading articles in which people said their memories had failed them, even after many abductions. It had been theorized that the aliens could actually erase memory. That people could be abducted dozens of times and, even aided by hypnotism, would have no conscious memory of what had transpired. Why, even Laura herself might already have been abducted, and simply couldn't remember. Her anger faded, and she felt considerably more hopeful.

"You must be hungry," she said.

"I guess I could eat something, yeah."

She stood to go down to the kitchen, but Bob took her hand in his, and lay his other hand, with great tenderness, on top of hers. She sat down again and remembered, many years ago, he had taken her hand just that same way standing beside Lake Michigan on a very cold but sunny day in April. They had gone to visit the Art Institute. It seemed like another life.

Now Bob was stroking her hand, looking at it with pleasure and curiosity, just the way Laura had imagined the aliens might. Outside the window spread the purple sky, empty except for a few pale stars.

Lisa Williams Kline

GUEST ROOM

When her daughter glided into the bedroom late that Friday night, Melissa wasn't asleep. A massive night sweat had awakened her only minutes before, and she was lying in the dark with the covers thrown back, fanning her pajama top dry.

"Mom, Leo is here," Nat said, coming around to Melissa's side of the bed. "I told him he could stay in our guest room."

"What?" Melissa pushed herself up on one elbow. Gradually the waves of Nat's blonde hair and the plunge of her white v-neck sweater materialized from the shadows. Jake stirred, breathed deeply in his sleep.

"He got kicked out of his apartment. He needs a place to stay."

"Natalie, no." Melissa felt for her glasses on the nightstand.

"Mom, he has nowhere to go."

"You've only known him for a week!"

"But, Mom, you said you wanted us to bring our friends over."

"Not at one-thirty in the morning to spend the night!"

"I won't let him try anything. Dad, please?"

"It's OK," Jake's voice came from the other side of the bed, muffled by the quilt.

"Jake!" Melissa sat up and punched him lightly on the shoulder.

"Ow!"

"We don't know anything about this boy!"

"Yes, you do!" Nat said. "Leo about peed his pants last night after all your questions. Mom, c'mon. You've met him. You've interrogated him. You know him."

Melissa *had* kind of grilled the boy, the same way Jake claimed her mother used to grill him. She'd managed to wring out of Leo that he'd come several years ago to North Carolina from a town close to Chernobyl in the Ukraine. He was now twenty and working as a cook in the restaurant where Nat was waitressing during her winter college break. He told Melissa he was hoping to start classes at the community college, and that he would be a U.S. citizen in a few months.

"We don't know his family," Melissa said. It sounded like what her mother used to say, but she was bothered by the way Leo's bloodshot eyes constantly swept the room, and the fact that he never smiled.

"Mom, you're such a snob!" Nat sounded like an echo of Melissa a few decades back.

"I'm not a snob, Natalie, I'm trying to use good judgment."

Jake lay his hand on her forearm. "Melissa, he's OK."

"Thanks, Dad." The glow of Nat's sweater floated from the room. Melissa heard murmuring in the family room, then the faint creak of the stairs.

She tossed her glasses back on the nightstand and lay back, her arms crossed over her chest. "Jake! I said 'no' and then you said 'yes.'"

Jake turned on his back, and sighed. "He's just a kid. Probably drunk, shouldn't drive."

"So we're inviting a drunk to spend the night in our house?"

"We're keeping a drunk off the streets. We're doing a mitzvah."

"We can't let him sleep across the hall from Nat. What if he sneaks into her bedroom in the middle of the night?"

"That's not going to happen." Jake turned onto his side, facing away from her.

"Well, we did it!"

"We were engaged. You had the hots for me."

She looked at the back of Jake's balding head in the gray grainy light. She did have the hots for him. Even now, she knew he still felt that way about her. This, she thought, was one of those miraculous things about life. "So…you don't think Nat has the hots for Leo?" she asked.

"Nope."

"How do you know?"

"Body language."

She processed this, pressed on. "He could overpower her."

"Nat's the strongest person in this house."

This was true. Nat worked out religiously, and could bench press more than Jake.

"In those action movies you always want to rent, Bruce Willis and Harrison Ford turn into weapons of mass destruction in order to protect their daughters. Let somebody threaten their daughter and those guys go ballistic."

Jake pulled the sheet halfway over his head. "I'm pacing myself."

"So you're not going up there."

"Not going up there."

They were silent for a few minutes. Melissa was thinking about Nat's uncompromising honesty and her passion for life. The intensity of Melissa's battles with Nat was matched only by the ferocity of her love for her. Melissa had often wished she could have as much will in her entire body as Nat had in her little finger. "Why did you say he could stay, Jake?"

Jake rolled back in her direction, pulled the sheet off his face. "Truth? Leo reminds me of my grandfather. I feel *nachus* for the kid."

Melissa stopped to consider. Jake's grandfather, Nathan, had fled Latvia in 1902 after being nearly kidnapped, with other Jewish boys, to march on the front lines of the Czar's army. Natalie was named after him. Melissa had seen pictures of him—small, wiry, pointed chin, slightly bent shoulders, but with a wolf-like longing in his eyes and an inscrutable smile. Jake had an audiotape of his grandfather telling the story about how he and his younger brother Max escaped by stowing away in the engine room of a cargo ship. Once in America, a middle-aged woman had allowed them to sleep in the back of her store for a few nights, until they could find work and a place to live.

"What if he's not like your grandfather at all? What if he's some kind of thief, or terrorist? What did he do to get kicked out of his apartment, anyway?"

Jake was silent.

"You're not going up there."

"Nope."

She raised her head and peeked over Jake's shoulder at the clock. Almost two. Her family had always been indecisive. For example, every few weeks for the past two years her father had said, "We're thinking of switching from Harris Teeter to Lowe's," and her mother had said, "But we're not sure," and so far nothing had happened. Her dad was a family practitioner, and there was the exciting dramatic medicine you see on TV, and then there was the medicine that her father practiced. "Give it tincture of time," he was fond of saying. "Sometimes the best thing to do is nothing."

Melissa was not free from the family curse. As a child she'd once stopped to pet a dog during a baseball game while running from third base to home. Being half-Welsh, Melissa had heaved a sigh of self-discovery and relief when she'd once heard a Welsh poet say, "The Welsh are a timid people." So her indecisiveness and timidity weren't completely her fault. They were hereditary!

She sat up, crossed her legs, and began energetically polishing her glasses lenses with the edge of the sheet. For four months now, Nat had experienced the hedonistic freedoms of dorm life. She'd been on her own, making decisions such as this every night. Also, in the movies, *everybody* sneaked down the hall into someone else's bedroom, right? There was the obligatory shot of him tiptoeing down the hall to her room...or her tiptoeing down the hall to his. This was always a romantic and charming scene.

Melissa hated the thought of having to be the bad guy— rigid, humorless, mistrustful, and not believing in love or spontaneity or any of those invisible things. She got up, put on her robe, and clomped up the stairs. Maybe Leo would decide to read the set of encyclopedias in her office before attacking Nat, and she'd arrive just in time.

Here was her bold plan: Her office was just down the hall from the guest room. She'd pretend to work on an article on charitable traditions in Christianity, Judaism, and Islam that she had to finish for work. The machine-gun sound of her fingers pounding the keyboard could stave off any number of unimaginable acts. They didn't say "The pen is mightier than the sword" for nothing.

Melissa passed the open door and empty bedroom of their younger daughter, Evie. Piles of clothes on the floor resembled a flock of lambs sleeping in the dark. Evie was spending the night at a friend's house. At the end of the hall was Nat's closed door and, directly across from it, the closed door of the guest room. This felt like "The Price is Right." What's behind Door Number 1?

Melissa pressed her ear up against Natalie's door.

The bed squeaked. Then groaned.

Her heart did calisthenics and a hot flash raced up her neck. She imagined herself throwing open the door, wild and powerful as a Valkyrie, with lightning bolts flashing from her eyes. Like that character from *The Matrix*, she'd be dressed in some tight-fitting black leather thing. She'd fly through the room executing amazing Kung Fu moves to flatten Leo against the wall just as he began to hunch over Nat. Melissa's maternal power would palpably snap through the air in an otherworldly way and Leo would crouch, trembling with fear, in the corner of the bedroom, wearing only his underwear, resembling Gollum from *The Lord of the Rings*.

Twin beads of sweat rolled out of her hair and down her temples and she mopped her soaking hairline with the sleeve of her pajama top. OK, maybe not.

She heard a sound from the guest room. Was it sobbing? No, laughing. She froze as the skin of her lower skull began to crawl. Somebody had turned on the TV. So they *were* in separate rooms. At least for now.

Loudly shuffling into her office, she reread the last few paragraphs she'd written for the article about charitable traditions. Observant Jews believed in "tikkun olam—" helping heal a broken world. Jesus taught Christians to follow his teachings by performing acts of kindness toward those in need. One of the five pillars of Islam was giving "zakat," or help to the poor.

But Melissa couldn't concentrate on the article. She typed "Ukraine" into her computer's search line. Around Chernobyl, people were dying of radiation-related cancers, and the soil would remain radioactive for at least fifty more years. No one could drink the water or even plant potatoes there. Due to deaths from Chernobyl, there were now thousands of orphans. Suddenly, Melissa remembered that's where her dentist, Dr. Hart, had gone, for three weeks last year, on a mission trip to fill cavities for the orphans. She'd told Melissa that the stress of the radioactive atmosphere broke down people's bodies, even their teeth. Melissa stared at photos of the children.

Leo did look a little unhealthy. Perhaps he was missing teeth, which might be a practical explanation for his close-lipped aversion to smiles.

And then she had an idea. A few times in the past, when Jake's snoring got loud enough to shake the tiles from the bathroom shower, she'd gone upstairs and crawled in bed with one of the girls. That's what she'd do. She'd just go get in Nat's bed. Later, if Leo tried to come in, she'd catch him red-handed.

Inspired, she pushed open Nat's bedroom door, and faint light from the hallway sliced a pie shape across the quilt, revealing Nat's curved back on the far side of her double bed, her hair tangled on the pillow. Nestled close to her was "Pink Blankey," her baby blanket, threadbare and impossibly soft from nineteen years of washing and snuggling. Quietly, Melissa pulled back the covers and slid onto the cool sheets next to her.

"What the hell are you doing?" Nat bolted upright. Pink Blankey became a deadly weapon, like the towels mean girls in junior high used to snap in the shower after gym. Nat shoved Melissa with her feet and, barely suppressing a groan, Melissa half-rolled, half-fell onto the floor. "I *told* you …" Nat went silent for a long moment.

Melissa lay completely still, her legs throbbing where Natalie had kicked her, a welt from the blanket burn starting to sizzle on her cheek.

"…Mom…?" Nat leaned down, touching her arm. "Oh, Mom! I'm so sorry, are you OK? Why were you getting in bed with me? I thought Leo was trying something. God, Mom, I am so sorry." She asked if Melissa was OK ten more times. She wrapped her in a hug and stroked her hair. "God, I tried to beat up my own mom with Pink Blankey! I feel so terrible! Man, it's a good thing I couldn't reach my mace."

Melissa straightened her bent glasses, kissed Nat good-night, and limped downstairs.

Melissa lay still and listened to the coffeemaker groan in the kitchen as Jake made coffee. Early in their marriage they'd joked that the coffeemaker sounded like it was having an orgasm. Sometimes just listening had been enough to send them back to bed.

"Breakfast!" Jake shouted. Melissa didn't move, but listened to his heavy footfalls as he climbed the stairs. He pounded like an army sergeant on both doors at the end of the hallway.

"Rise and shine."

Melissa got up, a bit gingerly, and put on some khakis and a sweater. She hoped Nat was kind enough not to mention their midnight wrestling match.

"That smells good," she told Jake as she came into the kitchen.

He cracked an egg into a bowl, and turned to kiss her.

"They up?" She took out four sets of utensils and napkins.

"*Now* they are. Separate bedrooms, by the way."

While she was setting the table the stairs creaked, and she glanced up to see Nat headed downstairs, wearing pajama pants and a sweatshirt, her eyes heavy with sleep, her hair tumbling in waves over her shoulders. Leo followed her, wearing one of Nat's sweatshirts, gray with "UNC" in sky-blue letters. It was only a bit snug.

"Good morning." Melissa reached deep to summon a welcoming smile.

"Morning!" Nat said brightly. "Leo, my dad makes the best breakfasts." She shot Melissa a rapid grin, and did a zipping motion across her lips.

"Morning," Leo said, avoiding Melissa's eyes, seeking Jake's. His skin was sallow, maybe from poor nutrition as a child. Or exposure to radiation as a young boy. Maybe they should encourage him to get a complete check-up.

"Leo, do you drink coffee?" she asked.

"No, ma'am, just milk, please."

Dr. Hart had told her that the cows had died from grazing on the radioactive soil. Milk was an enormous luxury. She took out one of her largest tumblers, and poured it full of pearly liquid.

Leo glanced at her furtively and she saw the rapid shift of his eyes and had a realization: He was afraid of her. Leo was afraid of *her*, the timid Welsh woman! This was so shocking she felt a hot flash coming on, sweeping across her scalp like wildfire in underbrush. Melissa quickly wiped the beads of sweat from her hairline before pouring another milk and two coffees.

"So, Leo, will you be going to school this semester?" she asked, as they all sat down.

"Watch out, Leo, my parents will feed you, but you have to keep answering all their questions about *your future*," Nat said, laughing.

Leo didn't smile. His face looked fearful and intense. "No, not this semester," he said. "My sister and father leave next week to return to Ukraine. So I will need to save my money a little longer."

"Have a bagel," said Jake. "These are the first decent bagels we've found down here."

"Thank you," said Leo.

"Why are your father and sister going back to the Ukraine?" Melissa asked.

"My sister doesn't like it here. My father, he has not been able to learn English."

"What about your mother?"

"She died of cancer long years ago."

"Oh, I'm so sorry." She looked at Jake as he assiduously piled lox onto his bagel. The poor boy had no mother. "So after they leave you'll be alone in the U.S.?"

"Yes, ma'am." Leo cleared his throat and shoveled a spoonful of eggs into his mouth. He did have bad teeth; Melissa caught a glimpse, and they were pointed and gray-looking. If he planned to stay in America he really should get caps or something. He would be competing for a job, a place in college and a mate against healthy American children with their bright white smiles.

Leo then turned to look at Nat and Melissa saw, not the wolf, but a dog-like devotion in his eyes. He was totally, helplessly smitten. His look was so naked that Melissa felt embarrassed for him. She felt close to tears.

She glanced at Jake again to see if he'd seen Leo's look but he was busy with his lox and bagels.

"Everything is very delicious, thank you," said Leo, nodding shyly.

"You're welcome any time, Leo," Melissa said. "Hey, why don't you come for dinner sometime this week?"

"That would be very nice," Leo said, with a smile of genuine feeling, she thought.

She smiled at Nat and Jake, hoping they'd be pleased that she'd finally been won over, but they were both focused on eating.

"How about Tuesday? Do you two have to work on Tuesday?"

"I think we do, Mom," Nat rose, waitress-like, to refill Jake's and Melissa's coffees.

"Well, Wednesday, then."

"Melissa, you're overwhelming the boy. He hasn't even finished this meal, and you're trying to get him to commit to another one," Jake said.

"I'd like to very much," Leo insisted, looking over at Nat, and back at Melissa, his small eyes welling.

Wednesday morning Melissa called Dr. Hart and told her about the young man who would soon be alone here.

"Did you say his father is going back next week?" When Melissa said that he was, Dr. Hart said, excited, "I'd like to send along some anesthesia. They're desperate for it there, and I found that the customs officials will look the other way."

"Anesthesia?" Melissa was confused. She'd thought Dr. Hart would want to help Leo.

"Yes," said Dr. Hart. "That boy, he's here, he's one of the lucky ones. Please let me know if the father is willing to take some."

"I will," Melissa said. "I'll get back to you."

Around lunchtime, as Melissa was emailing her editor the last few changes to the article on charitable traditions, Nat came into her office.

"So," Melissa said, still typing, looking at Nat over her glasses. "What do you think Leo likes? Daddy said he could make steaks on the grill tonight. Leo looks like he could use some red meat."

Nat twisted her hair up into one of the messy buns popular among girls her age. "Forget it, Mom. You're not going to turn Leo into some project. Besides, he's a loser."

"A loser?" Melissa repeated. "He came here from the Ukraine, he learned English, he's becoming a citizen and earning money to go to college, he's going to stick it out here all by himself when the rest of his family is going back. I don't call that a loser at all." Leo really was amazingly similar to Jake's grandfather, she'd decided.

"He's not saving to go to college. And I found out yesterday that he's not becoming an American citizen. That was a lie, too."

"What do you mean?" Melissa couldn't believe it.

"He just said all that to impress me, I guess."

"Oh." Melissa hesitated. She felt a little betrayed, yet, she could see how a boy, feeling desperate, might embellish the truth. "He likes you a lot, I could see it in his eyes."

"Well, then he should have told me the truth, then."

Melissa's whole body felt heavier. Poor Leo!

Seconds ticked by.

"Don't you think I used good judgment, the way you and Dad taught me to?"

"Well..." Melissa looked up at Nat's passionate face, her mouth open to speak, but without a ready answer. That was, indeed, exactly what they had taught her to do.

Nat gently touched the welt on Melissa's cheek, almost gone now. "God, I still can't believe I tried to beat you up with Pink Blankey." She hesitated, then patted Melissa's arm. "But see, Mom, I'm a big girl, I can take care of myself."

"I see." Melissa laughed, though tears welled at the edge of her eyes. They had taught her that, too.

Natalie glanced at the digital clock on her phone. "I promised Terri I'd meet her at the mall. And we'll probably pick up something to eat there." When she leaned to kiss Melissa good-bye her hair smelled like coconut. "Love you, Mom."

"Love you, too, sweetie."

After Nat left Melissa called Jake at work. "No need to pick up steaks, unless you want to fix them for you and me and Evie. Leo's not coming."

"See?" Jake laughed.

"You're enjoying saying 'I told you so.' Do I sense any regret?"

"A little."

"He is like your grandfather," she said. "I kind of fell for him."

"And he'll survive by his own wits, Melissa, just like my grandfather. I always loved what my grandfather said on that tape. He said, 'When I came to America, I didn't know an orange from an apple, but I became a fruit vendor.' Remember that Yiddish accent? I could almost see the way he gestured when he said it, like he was holding an apple, holding the key to life."

She remembered.

Lisa Williams Kline

"Hey, you know what, I'll get steaks anyway," Jake said. "For you and me and Evie."

"OK," Melissa said, and placed the phone gently back in its cradle.

ORNAMENT CUSTODY

The winter after my divorce I lived on cigarettes and Chardonnay. One windy Saturday afternoon, three days before Christmas, I was at the kitchen table in my soft, worn flannel pajamas, cuddling my new cat, Cleo, when my friend Cheryl called me.

I pictured Cheryl in her bare kitchen. Also in her late twenties, recently divorced and without children, she was determined to save both herself and me. "I'm taking you to get a Christmas tree," she announced.

"Oh, no." Buying a Christmas tree, lugging it home, and decorating it felt like solving world hunger or climbing Everest. I blew a gray smoke cloud against the window and watched it billow back at me, relieved to be able to support my hometown, Winston-Salem, even if I had failed at everything else.

"I'll be there in half an hour," Cheryl said. "Be ready." Cheryl's father had been in the military. Inertia was not her friend.

By the time she arrived I had rejected several outfits based on the fact that they were either in the laundry, covered with cat hair, or too much trouble to put on. I had brushed Cleo's soft calico fur and lit another cigarette for further contemplation but that was all I had accomplished.

Cheryl's frosted hair was pulled into a severe career-woman's ponytail. A UCLA sweatshirt hung on her scarecrow-like frame. Her husband had left in May, mine in August. Neither of us had eaten a decent meal since. "Lisa! Get with it, girl! I'm taking you to get a Christmas tree, dammit!"

Cleo laid back her translucent ears, leaped from my lap and scrambled under the couch. Her yellow eyes followed Cheryl.

"Do you think he has a Christmas tree?" I wondered.

"Oh, for Crissake, if he does, who cares? You never loved him anyway." Cheryl, after forcing me to admit this terrible truth, then forced me into a pair of ill-fitting jeans and the passenger seat of her Mazda RX-7. I hadn't been out of the house in awhile and the frigid wind lashed tears to my eyes.

"Face it, Lisa, you yourself admitted you were still on the rebound from your college boyfriend when you settled for him. Well, you and I, we're not settling—ever again."

"Right," I said. People always asked us if we were sisters. This puzzled me. Cheryl is almost six feet tall, a veritable vortex of authority. I am barely five feet tall and routinely allow people to break in line in front of me. Our only similarities are the ubiquitous cigarettes and the frosted shade of our hair.

On the way to the tree lot Cheryl began one of her immensely entertaining stories. While never actually lying, she had a special gift for dramatic embellishment. "So after this particular boyfriend left, I was broke. He took everything. Until I got my first paycheck all I could afford was eggs. For two weeks, all I ate was eggs."

"Eggs? For two weeks?"

"Yes, eggs."

"Not a single leaf of lettuce or piece of cheese."

"Egg-zactly."

"Wow." Larry, too, had taken everything, mostly because I felt so very guilty for not loving him. I had shoved it all on him — cars, lamps, rugs, even the dog. He refused to take the house because he had recently refinanced it for more than it was worth.

Cheryl squealed into the tree lot and the Mazda lurched to a stop. I followed her over to the stand where the tree salesman in a gray hooded sweatshirt hovered over a space heater. "How much is your very best tree?"

The salesman pointed at a magnificent blue-green specimen. "Seventy-five dollars."

I grimaced. Then Cheryl spotted a waif-like bush that could have starred in a Charlie Brown special. Its trunk took off at an angle. It looked like a beaver had flossed with most of the branches on one side.

"You could put that side up against the wall," Cheryl whispered, then added loudly, "Most people already have their trees."

"You don't," the tree man pointed out.

"How much is it?" I asked.

"Twenty-five dollars."

Cheryl slapped her knee as if he had told the world's funniest joke. "That's the most pitiful-looking tree I've ever seen. Who would ever buy it?"

"You."

"We'll give you ten dollars for it."

The man chewed on his mustache and shrugged. "OK."

"I don't even want a tree." This all seemed so very pointless. I longed to go back to my kitchen, smoke another cigarette, sink the tips of my fingers into Cleo's soft, soft fur, and pour cold chardonnay into a thin-stemmed glass. "I guess I can put that side up against the wall," I added, after Cheryl glared at me.

The hooded tree-man shouldered our Charlie Brown special, but when he saw the Mazda two-seater he blinked hard. "How to you plan to get this tree home?"

"Piece of cake." Cheryl proceeded to amaze the tree man by lowering the roof and back vinyl window of the Mazda, partially by power button, and partially by hand. "Lisa, you can hold the tree in your lap while I drive."

So I did. The wind chill must have been minus 100, and my skin crawled with being pricked by thousands of frozen green needles. The tree completely obliterated my view of the outside world and any view the outside world might have had of me. As far as anyone passing us was concerned, Cheryl was out for a drive in dangerously cold weather with a tree.

A few hours later we agreed the tree didn't look so bad in my living room with the bald spot facing the wall. I climbed the attic stairs and retrieved the box of Christmas ornaments I had been collecting for the last three or four years.

Larry liked salt-water aquariums, and one year I'd made a half-dozen tropical fish ornaments out of salt dough. I'd researched them thoroughly—I can still remember the queen angel and the yellow tang. My grandmother had crocheted and starched a box of white snowflakes. Friends and family had given me an eclectic collection of cat ornaments, and for the top I had a white peacock with a fantastical tail.

Cleo wiggled underneath the tree skirt, stalked the blinking lights, chewed the needles, and played soccer with a papier-maché cat. This was definitely the most fun she'd had since I'd adopted her.

Cheryl and I went for an early dinner after finishing the lights. She was in a hurry when she dropped me off because she had a date later. I thanked her for jolting me from my self-pitying stupor, and waved to her, as she screeched around the corner, with a jauntiness I hadn't felt in months. When I reached out to slide my key in the lock,

I saw that the light was on in the living room and the door was slightly ajar. Someone was in my house.

With a quick intake of breath, I placed my hand on the knob and slowly pushed the door inward. I stepped inside, and nearly collided with Larry on his way out, carrying a cardboard box.

"What are you doing here/" My heart heaved and I felt the tingle of racing adrenalin.

"I'm taking my half," he said. He wore an ancient argyle sweater of his father's I'd always hated. His auburn hair was limp and unclean, his freckles were ghostly pale. He was so thin his Adam's apple looked like a knife edge, and there was a bloody piece of toilet paper stuck to it where he'd cut himself shaving.

"Your half of what?" My voice was very loud, a combination of adrenalin and wine from dinner.

"The Christmas ornaments," he said. I focused on the box in his arms. Nestled in tissue paper were all of the fish ornaments.

"I made those!"

"You made them for me, they're mine," he shouted. "You loved me once!"

I glimpsed several of my grandmother's starched snowflakes. "You can't have my grandmother's snowflakes!"

"She told me I was a fine young man!"

"She didn't mean it!"

"Yes, she did!"

"She was my grandmother—I ought to know how she felt! She made these for me, not you!" I reached for the box, he tried to yank it from my hand, and slung the ornaments across the room.

There was a sort of snapping explosion in my head.

"Get out of here!" someone screamed, and Larry was backing out the door because someone was punching and slapping him. The person had to be me, a fact my brain registered with more than faint surprise.

"I'm changing the locks!" I shouted as he sprinted down the block to where he'd parked his car. I slammed the door and leaned on it, then sank down to the floor. I had not loved him once, not ever, but I'd made everyone think I did, including myself. I crawled around the room, picking up broken ornaments and wiping my slippery face with the back of my hand.

Cleo ventured from under the couch. She sniffed the broken fish on the floor and rubbed up against my arm. She touched her nose to my wet, salty cheek, then licked it.

I glued the fish back together and while they dried on the kitchen counter I hung my grandmother's crocheted snowflakes on Charlie Brown's half-eaten branches. I plugged in the tree lights. They leaped to colorful brilliance, outlining a shape that was definitely more perfect than the tree itself. When all the ornaments were hung I sat in the dark with Cleo on my lap, admiring the beauty I had imparted to that pitiful tree by all my work.

I felt I had made a breakthrough of sorts and ceremonially flushed the rest of my cigarettes down the toilet before going to bed. In the middle of a sensuous dream about my college boyfriend begging me to take him back I awoke to a loud crash.

Was Larry back? I sat upright, instantly alert, and remained still, listening. I heard only a faint tinkling noise. The digital clock glowed 4:22. I tiptoed to the landing and peeked into the living room below.

My tree was prone on the floor, a tangle of twisted lights, snapped branches, and re-broken ornaments. Cleo was crouched in the middle of it all, batting a broken fish-head with her soft white paw. She looked up at me and I swear she was smiling.

Wearily, I sat on the top step, my head clanging from too much wine. What difference would it make if I just left the mess until morning? Who cared, really, if I left it for a week? I ignored the sludge of defeat that had begun to ooze through my bones. With grim determination, I pulled Charlie Brown upright. Pine needles rained down and the water in the tree stand soaked the carpet. The lights were so tangled I had to take them off and start again. The fish ornaments had broken again, all in the same places. I re-glued them. While waiting for them to dry, I searched every drawer in the house, without success, for any cigarettes I might have missed in my zeal for reform. By sunrise I had restrung the light, re-glued and re-hung the ornaments, and vacuumed.

The next night, Cleo, apparently pleased that I had restored her plaything to its previous state, climbed the tree again. Again I had it back up by dawn. Then I shoved her carrying case in the back seat for the seven-hour drive to my parents' house in Winston-Salem for Christmas. I stopped and picked up my grandmother in Richmond on the way, and put her old navy-blue suitcase on the back seat beside Cleo. Mom hates cats, and made Cleo say in the basement, and whenever I went downstairs to visit her I sneaked one of the cigarettes I had bought at the gas station on the way down while my grandmother was in the Ladies' Room.

Cheryl and I have both remarried and our kids went to camp together. We both quit smoking years ago. Our friendship has evolved into a sisterhood and I like to hope that over the years I have helped her as much as she has helped me. I hear that Larry has married and divorced again. My grandmother broke my heart when she died a month after I remarried. Cleo ran out in front of a car that very same week, which I prefer to think was purely coincidental. Cheryl is still gifted with a flair for dramatic storytelling; in her version of the story, Cleo pulled down my tree for 12 nights in a row. Hearing this, our families roar with glee.

My husband is Jewish, but we have a prenuptial agreement that we will always have a Christmas tree. Most years, it's a joyous ritual. Sometimes it's a labor of grim determination. But we haven't missed a year.

BLACK AND BLUE

Pam was quite sure she was the only one in the stadium who recognized the author. She hadn't wanted to come to this cheerleading competition with her daughter; earlier today she'd tried to get out of it, mentioned a deadline for the library newsletter, a friend Lauren could ride with, but one look at Lauren's thin freckled face and she had stuffed her notebook into her purse, and said, "Of course I'm coming, I just might need to do a little work, that's all."

And while descending the shallow concrete steps in the small stadium, after leaving Lauren practicing in a field outside with the rest of her squad, Pam saw the author. She recognized her face from the book jacket. It was only because Pam worked part-time in a quiet branch library, and spent her spare minutes reading, gazing at author photos in an attempt to osmose their lives, and toiling over her own plodding attempts at storytelling, did she recognize the lovely prominent cheekbones, the distinctive Semitic nose, the hooded, haunted eyes.

She sat thin and alone in a timeless gray sweater among the loud, brightly clad cheerleading parents and coaches, like a sparrow among blue jays and peacocks. Pam herself wore a blue T-shirt that said WILDCAT PRIDE, as well as a large pin with her daughter's photo proclaiming her to be "Proud Cheerleading Mom." In addition to her daughter's Power Bars, she also carried two empty plastic bottles filled with dried beans that she had been instructed to wave with hysterical fervor when her daughter's squad took the stage. God help her, she planned to shake those dried beans. As if her life depended upon it.

The author had been raised in the tightrope world of southern Judaism, had during her early professional life worked on Capital Hill, and in fact had been a commentator on Washington events for public television. In the past two decades she had retired to a rural North Carolina town to write, turning down all interview and appearance requests. Her only novel had been released about three years ago, and it had been deemed by the New York Times Book Review to be "A geography of Southern Jewish life with the romping surrealist absurdity of *A Confederacy of Dunces*." It had won a number of prestigious prizes. However, perhaps because of the author's refusal to make appearances, it had lackluster sales and Pam had seen it soon thereafter at a used book store on the remainder table.

There was a passage in that book that Pam had never forgotten, about a girl and her sick mother living together, and the girl running away for the whole day, and finally, after coming close to leaving altogether, returning at dusk. Her mother never said a word, had, in truth, wished for her daughter to claim her freedom without holding her back. The mother had left a cold plate of food on the table.

These thoughts tumbled through Pam's consciousness like a frenetic fast-forward montage in the five seconds it required to walk by the author. She slipped into a seat next to the father of her daughter's best friend.

"Hey, Pam." Dwight was lanky, good-natured, and baby-faced, and always wore a NASCAR cap.

"Hey, Dwight. Are we gonna win today or what?" Not many dads attended these day-long, sometimes weekend long cheerleading events. Pam's husband, Ben, a pilot for World Airways, flew sometimes for three weeks at a time, and hadn't attended any competitions all year. But Dwight, who worked on a NASCAR pit crew, had two cheerleading daughters, and had immersed himself in the sport. His wife usually accompanied the younger daughter to her competitions, and he came to Shelby's. He knew how many points would be deducted for a fall, for a knee touching the floor, for a foot slipping outside the competition area, for an incorrect release. He knew how many points the team could earn with each perfectly executed back-handspring-back-tuck, each lay-out, each full, each double-up, double-down, scorpion, or bow-and-arrow.

Dwight grinned. "Greenwood can beat our butts if we don't hit everything. Last year we only beat 'em by two points. You better believe this year they want to beat us *ba-ad*."

Over the red peak of Dwight's Nascar cap, Pam sneaked a glance at the author. How ironic that a notoriously reclusive intellectual, so private, so opposed to fanfare, would be at a cheerleading competition, a place where the entire *raison d'etre* was to make an enormous fuss. In this venue, she was invisible in plain sight.

"I forgot to give Lauren her water bottle, be right back," she said to Dwight. "You want me to take anything to Shelby?"

"Yeah, let me give you a couple dollars so she can get a drink from the machine." Dwight handed Pam the money. "Miss Bebe said they'd look for a practice field behind the concession stand." Pam climbed the shallow cement steps. As she approached the author she slowed, noting the small wire-rimmed glasses and ancient blue jeans, as faded as a sky before snow. She was reading a fat paperback with chunks of print that seemed to be essays, but Pam couldn't see the cover. Her worn tan suede walking shoes reminded Pam of trembling rabbits hiding in the grass.

At the top of the stadium steps, Pam pretended to be looking for someone, and turned to scan the audience, just to glimpse again the small, neat bun at the nape of the author's neck. Of her novel the Los Angeles Times reviewer had written, "Hugely discomforting and affecting; a hilarious yet searing portrait of modern southern Jewish life."

Pam wanted to tell her that the scene with the girl and her mother had been so vivid, so affectingly rendered, that when the girl saw the plate of cold food on the table Pam had spontaneously burst into tears. Once as a child of ten she had run away for a day and her parents had either pretended not to notice or been so busy they truly hadn't realized she was gone. When she returned at the end of a soul-searching and mostly hunger-inducing trek in the woods nothing had been said but "Wash your hands and eat." Somehow with that single scene the author had captured the world of Pam's childhood.

In the novel the author had also fictionalized her experiences as a Duke freshman during the High Holy Days, when she taught half a dozen Jewish girls the proper way to fast on Yom Kippur. Her hall mates had grown up in Pittsburgh, Philadelphia, and New York, surrounded by Jewish culture, but they had somehow been less knowledgeable about the exact nature of the rules governing fasting. She had stood in front of the water fountain, saying, "No! Not even water!" while parched and cranky girls had shoved her aside and chugged the cool water like beer.

At Duke, Pam had fallen in love with a Jewish boy two years ahead of her who, like the author, was serious about fasting. He believed that denying yourself was a purifying experience. She steeped herself in Jewish culture, reading everything she could find, even considered conversion, but her boyfriend had finally explained to her, a few days before he graduated, that nothing could ever come of their relationship. He never put it into so many words, but Pam eventually came to understand that for him denying her was a purifying experience not unlike fasting on Yom Kippur. After that, she had gone through a period of denial herself, feeling that only one day of fasting was nothing; she could do much, much better than that. She showed the world, in the year that followed, just how purifying self-control could be. When her roommate dragged her to student health the next February, she had shingles and weighed less than ninety pounds. The resident who admitted Pam was irate. She raged at the course loads, the high expectations of the professors, the pressure to achieve at the Harvard of the south. Pam let her believe it.

Over the next five years she eked her way back to health, found a quiet career at the library, and met Ben. Even though the relationship with the Jewish boy had ended over twenty years ago, she still devoured novels like this particular author's, exploring the strange otherness, the simultaneous feelings of inferiority and superiority, and the mysteries of fasting and feasting.

Behind the stadium, she wandered from one damp field to another, searching for her daughter's squad. Liquid silver Rorschach mirages dotted the parking lot and steam rose from the grass. It was going to be one of those sweltering days in September where everyone yearned for a whisper of fall.

On the way to the competition, Lauren hyperventilated. Pam kept paper bags in the car for just such events. When they arrived, Lauren threw up, as always. It was in the parking lot, thank goodness, and not in the car, and didn't get on her uniform. Once a girl threw up in the middle of the dance and for the entire two and a half minute routine the others slid across the floor in her vomit. At the end of that same routine another girl fell on her face and broke her nose. Amazingly, the squad had still come in second in their division.

Lauren's squad members had made more trips to the emergency room than members of the school's football team. For broken elbows, broken noses, broken ankles, teeth knocked out, and concussions. It was more than fitting that their team colors were black and blue.

Besides Dwight, Pam could never remember the other parents' names. For three years now she'd thought, "She'll outgrow this, she'll move into something that's more meaningful, like the school newspaper or the student Habitat for Humanity Club." This was a far cry from the days of Pam's youth, when a gaggle of sexually aggressive girls waved pom-poms on the football or basketball sidelines, chanting,

> *Pork chops, pork chops, greasy, greasy.*
> *We can beat your team easy, easy*

More than once she'd been told by other parents that her daughter was extremely gifted. Lauren was one of the feather-light, petite girls who let themselves be tossed in the air or held by their ankles while they struck soaring swan-like poses. Girls in Lauren's position had to be tiny but they also had to have an incredible amount of faith that someone down below was going to catch them. "She's the best flyer on the squad, you know that, right?" other parents would say.

And Pam thought, "Best at what? Standing on tiptoe on someone else's hands? Falling from someone's shoulders into someone else's arms? If only you could have seen the painting she did of her father in his flight uniform when she was only ten. Now *that* was talent." But Lauren didn't paint anymore, she cheered.

But Pam had to admit that the first time she'd watched the squad compete, Lauren's limber little body had been pirouetted skyward by four pairs of hands, and the look she'd thrown the audience as she reached the peak and spread her arms like wings—Pam learned later the correct term was "facial"—had been saucy, defiant, and joyous. To be honest Pam had been intensely moved; she'd felt metaphorically transported to the end of the first act of *Peter Pan*. There was something seductively invincible about figuring out a bona fide way to fly. For a few seconds Laura broke free of everything, and, as Pam watched, her heart soared with her daughter.

She came upon Lauren's squad, the slim cylinders of their bodies ramrod straight in military formation. Their hair was tightly braided back like French schoolchildren and their blue and black polyester uniforms fit like second skins. Their shining cheeks seemed to have sprouted newly sharp cheekbones, just as their hips had recently formed faint curves and their chests bloomed bee-stung breasts. They were executing standing back tucks on command.

"Again!" shouted Miss Bebe, the coach, a diminutive brassy-haired woman from Alabama who had been rumored to be the best cheerleading coach in the area, having taken the squad to a national championship the year before. "You'll do it until every single one of you lands it!"

Again and again, they leapt up into the air, curled backward into fetal balls, and landed on their feet.

"That looked like crap! Again! Now, stick it, ladies!"

Someone always wobbled, stumbled, fell to one knee. One girl fell on her chin, but thankfully they were on grass and instead of a crimson gush there was only a smear of green.

Lauren's face was a mask of agony; her body as thin as a pencil. She had landed every back tuck so far but Pam knew that if they had to do many more she, too, would stumble. She was closing her eyes before each one, silently begging for the rest of the girls to do it right. Pam closed her eyes and begged for it too.

Lisa Williams Kline

After fifteen minutes they were all winded and trembling and still they hadn't succeeded. *Please, stop. They'll be too tired to compete.*

"If that Greenwood team came out here to watch y'all, they'd start laughing," Miss Bebe yelled. "Girls, I'm ashamed to be your coach. I really am."

Just when Pam thought she couldn't watch another second, and turned to walk away, Miss Bebe gave the girls a break. Pam handed the water bottle to Lauren and the money to Shelby.

"Mom, you're not supposed to watch," Lauren said, her chest heaving, white spots on her cheeks. She almost never ate anything. Pam tried to find foods that were appealing. She tried not to nag. One of the other flyers had developed an eating disorder and she didn't want it to happen to Lauren.

"Y'all are looking really good. Drink some water," Pam said. "Shelby, you be sure and get something to drink."

"Yes, ma'am," Shelby said, dabbing the sweat from her face with her fingers and then swiping the skirt of her uniform. "It's sooo hot."

"I'm about to die," Lauren said.

"Ladies, back to work!" When Miss Bebe clapped her hands it sounded like gunshots. She pointed a red nail at Pam. "Bye, mom!"

Obediently, Pam walked away. Lauren, in formation, did not turn her head to watch her go. Pam headed back to the stadium seats, letting her thoughts float to other places.

Maybe the author would be making her way out to buy a snack before the competition began and Pam would happen to say, "Oh! Pardon me. By the way, I have no wish to intrude, of course, but may I say that I found your book to be profoundly *resonant*."

Perhaps the author would duck her head and smile in a bashful way and say, "Why, thank you, what a delight to meet one of the five people who read it."

Perhaps the author would invite Pam to join her for a bag of peanuts, and while waiting in line at the concession stand somehow they'd begin to discuss narrative structure or objective correlative and the author would be pleased, in a weary way. "Imagine finding a kindred soul at a cheerleading competition," she'd say, adjusting her glasses, perhaps squinting at Pam a bit more closely.

Of course none of this happened.

She rejoined Dwight. Blaring rap music thundered from the stage, and the master of ceremonies bounded out, wearing a muscle shirt and tights, shouting into a handheld mike. "Ladies and gentlemen, girls and boys, put your hands together and make some noise, welcome to the Universal Spirit National Cheerleading Competition!"

Dwight jumped to his feet and let out a wolf whistle. "Yeah! Let's go, WILDCATS!" The other parents around Pam jumped to their feet as well, whooping and shaking the plastic bottles of beans like restless natives in a National Geographic documentary. Pam stood. Twice, she shook her beans.

She glanced over at the author. As the deafening roar swelled around her, the author marked the place in her book with a studied reverence, abandoning her reading with obvious regret. Pam wondered what team her daughter or granddaughter was on. Then she noticed a round green and yellow pin on her gray sweater. Greenwood! The reclusive author was an arch-rival!

"In this competition," Dwight said, leaning close and cupping a warm damp hand over Pam's ear so she could hear over the noise, "we get five points for audience participation."

"You're kidding," she said.

"Serious as a heart attack," he said, adjusting his toothpick, and then his cap. "Our girls are gonna need us *ba-ad* today. Yessirree. Those five points could mean the championship." He glanced at his watch. "In about ten minutes the girls'll go back stage and Coach Bebe will give us a brief lesson on what to do."

"Don't we just yell loud?"

"Oh, no! It's very important *when* we yell and *what* we yell. And when we're quiet. Kinda like doing a responsive reading in church on Sunday."

"I can never do those right," she admitted.

"Well, today you gotta do it right cause it's worth five points," he said.

"Then bring it on," she said grimly. She supposed the reclusive author would be trying to earn five points as well. It was impossible for Pam to imagine her jumping up and down, screaming and waving a bottle of beans.

The parents gathered round Miss Bebe in a secret location behind the restroom with their bottles of beans, and their black-and-blue attire, their chests festooned with pins. Coach Bebe regarded them, hands on hips. "All right, Moms...and Dwight—" Coach Bebe flashed Dwight a sexy smile, "Let's see if you can do this. And make it *sharp*. Here's how it goes:

Who's blue? We are!

Who's black? We are, we are!

Blue, black!

Blue, black!

Moms, I cannot tell you how much these five points are going to matter. Greenwood is awesome. I saw them practicing backstage, and this is the honest to God truth, ya'll, they *rock*. Moms..." She flashed another sexy smile. "And Dwight. This is *huge*."

Pam followed Dwight back to their seats. "So, you think you can handle it?" he said.

"Dwight, come on, I went to a four-year college. I think I can do a cheer." Pam was worried, though. She had always been one of those people who at the moment of truth get panic anxiety and screw up simple endeavors like punching buttons. She would never have been able to punch that button to save humanity the way Bruce Willis did at the end of *Armageddon*. For example, she had accidentally erased the video of her wedding to Ben a month after the ceremony while trying to make a copy for someone. It had been sixteen years and she still hadn't had the guts to tell Ben. Fortunately, she had lucked out; in sixteen years, Ben had never asked to view that particular piece of tape.

One of the clever things about cheerleading competitions is that there are many, many divisions. This means many competitors go home happy champions, and return to compete again next year. And sponsors go home happier and richer. Thus, there was only one squad other than Lauren's competing in their division: Greenwood.

And Greenwood was first.

The house went dark. Strobe lights swept the blue mats, circled the ceiling, and Greenwood, like parakeets in their green and yellow uniforms, bounded out to deafening applause. Their routine started out with the first three notes of "She's So Fine." Two girls crossed in diagonals across the stage, tumbling like jacks.

"Kick fulls," said Dwight, his elbows on his knees, watching and nodding. "Backwards lay-outs. Damn. Cross tumbling passes with two fulls and a punchfront to a double."

Now the rest of the Greenwood squad bounded onto the stage, went into formation with five stunt groups, and reeled off pike basket tosses, heel stretches - with loud bell-ringing sound effects—scorpions, and bows and arrows. The music was thundering, eyeball-scorching loud. The Greenwood squad hit their ending pyramid to thunderous applause.

Dwight leaned back with a soft whistle, adjusting his Nascar cap. "Not too shabby. We got our work cut out for us, I tell you what."

Pam glanced at the author. She stood quietly, watching. But she did have a bemused, proud look on her angular face. She seemed to be focusing on a sturdy girl with excited eyes and a wild ponytail of mahogany ringlets. She was a base, one of the girls who had to lift weights to maintain their strength, who kept both feet firmly planted to throw and catch the little ones. One of the ones you had to depend on.

The stage went dark. Lauren's squad was up. Oh God. A ghostly voice on the tape said, "Are you scared?" And, after a breathless beat, music crashed from the ceiling and Wildcat tumblers careened from the four corners like dervishes, whipping out athletic round-off back-handsprings and front flips with 360 degree twists, heightened with sound effects of the cracking of whips. Shelby was one of the girls performing the opening tumbling passes, and Dwight gripped the brim of his cap with both hands, holding his breath, then cried "Thank you Jesus!" as she landed without a flaw. The parents were on their feet screaming and shaking their beans. Pam's throat hurt and her heart hit her chest like a wrestling ref pounding his hand on the mat.

The rest of their girls bounded onstage, and the entire squad in formation opened with that dreaded standing back tuck. Every girl hit it except Lauren, who fell to one knee. Pam wanted to cry. Not many points would be deducted for just one knee touching, but she already suspected, no matter what happened for the rest of the routine, Lauren would cry to the point of hiccups and exhaustion all the way home. And she would go to bed and refuse food until tomorrow morning when perhaps Ben, if he made it home, could persuade her to eat an egg.

But the show had to go on. The squad went into their full-ups and their stretch double downs and Lauren jackknifed through the air like a hummingbird, then hit her bow-and-arrow and her arabesque on the money, her sweet shining face suffused with joy. She never showed her inner defeat. Her hardest move was the double-down, where she pulled her heel to her skull in a scorpion pose and then completed two full twists on the way down.

"Perfect," said Dwight, with a nod of approval. And now the responsive reading. The girls stood in rows, holding up signs that said "Blue," and "Black."

"Let's do it," said Dwight, punching Pam's arm.

Everyone else began to shout their lines. Pam had decided that due to her lack of talent, the best way for her to contribute to the five points would be to lip synch. Anything she shouted could and would be used against her. She could be the Milli Vanilli of cheerleading. But now, since Lauren's knee had touched, she had to help her. She had to abandon her Milli Vanilli plan. She screamed her throat raw. "Blue! Black! Blue! Black!"

"Pam, great job!" Dwight said when they finished, giving her a hearty thumbs' up.

Pam smiled modestly. "Thanks."

Their squad hit their ending pyramid, with Lauren at the very top. The music built to an explosive crescendo, and Lauren soared upward, as if she might blast straight through the roof of the hall. Then she dove with a whip-like double twist, like a spiraling fighter jet in her black and blue, into her bases' arms.

It was over.

Dwight and Pam collapsed into their seats, breathless.

"Damn near perfect," he said, shaking his head, his arms crossed over his chest. "Lauren's knee touching on that standing back tuck is the only thing I saw. Let's hope the judges didn't see it." He grinned, showing the gap in his teeth again.

Of course the judges saw it. They were trained to see everything.

Now there would be a short break, during which time the judges would compile the points. "Lemme go find Shelby," Dwight said. Pam told him to tell Lauren she'd be there in a minute.

Now was her chance. She stepped across the wide cement aisle and approached the reclusive author. "Excuse me," Pam said. "I loved your book."

She squinted up at Pam and gave her a small smile, with a faint expression of dread, touching an index finger to the corner of one wire rim. "Thank you."

"It spoke to me," Pam added. "It helped me make sense of my life."

"I'm glad." She smiled, then looked away. Her eyes found those of her daughter or granddaughter, who now bounded up the aisle in her green and yellow, her curly ponytail bouncing. Both of their faces sparked with unconcealed joy as she stood to hug her.

And so Pam went to take Lauren a snack. She found her lined with the rest of her squad in the flattened grass.

"You all looked like crap!" Miss Bebe was shouting.

"No you didn't," Pam said to Lauren. "You were wonderful. Absolutely wonderful."

Lauren's face shone.

"You'll keep doing them until every single one of you lands it," Miss Bebe finished. "Again!"

And all of them threw themselves backwards, into thin air, headfirst and with absolute faith, into one of those tortured fetal balls. But this time—like a miracle—every last one of those girls landed on her feet.

BLIZZARD BABIES
(A true story)

I had just delivered Caitlin, my first child, via C-section, and had been scheduled to take her home, but when I woke, the view from my hospital room revealed a white parking lot with snow so deep the cars were unidentifiable humps, like mattress batting.

"Lisa?" My husband Jeff called, his voice cracked with stress. "I'm going to try to dig the car out but I have no idea how long it will take."

"Oh, I can't stay another day!" I couldn't stand the antiseptic smells, the groans of pain, the cold floors, the endless waiting for someone to bring you something. Not to mention the nurses yelling at me for my maternal incompetence. I'd been stuck here for three days, waiting. Last night, my doctor had finally signed the release form. Now this.

"I'll try," Jeff said. "No guarantees."

I trundled dejectedly down the corridor, taking tiny steps to protect my incision, the kind of steps young Chinese girls centuries ago with bound feet might have taken. I wanted my own bed, my own shower, my own couch. I wanted to dress Caitlin in the little clothes I had folded so neatly in the white dresser. Experienced mothers with older children had told me that the second time around, I'd invent ailments to stay longer. Maybe. Right now, I wanted to take my baby and go home.

I glanced into a room as I passed and saw a guy with an unsettling resemblance to my ex-husband. On the phone, standing next to a bed with a blond woman in it. He even had a similar insistent, cajoling tone to his voice.

"Lydia! You sound fabulous as usual, can you put me through to Jim?"

I took a good look. Good God, it WAS my ex-husband. I dashed past the doorway and out of his sight, instigating a searing pain suggesting that I had torn my incision, then leaned against the wall to catch my breath. I hadn't seen Reid in almost three years—with no children there had been no reason for contact—but I'd heard from mutual friends that he was still in the area and had remarried. A blast of emotion triggered simultaneous waterfalls of adrenalin, breast milk and cold sweat.

What the hell was he doing here? Did he have a new baby too?

Dazed, I limped to the nursery. A faint rhythmic throbbing had begun around my incision. I extended my wrist so the nurse could compare my bracelet to Caitlin's. Caitlin was asleep, her tiny nearly translucent fingers folded under her chin beneath the edge of the tightly swaddled blanket.

How was I going to get Caitlin back to my room without going back by Reid's?

I read the names printed on the ends of the bassinettes as I wheeled Caitlin by the bundled babies behind the picture window. Some lay in quiet wonder, some flailed, others were in varying stages of sleep. And there it was. "Byer," the last name that had been mine for four years. Inside was a long, thin, wailing baby.

Even at one day old, there was a resemblance. A baby that could have been mine but, by a twist of fate, was not.

OK, I would speed-walk by his room, turning my face away so he wouldn't recognize me. Setting my jaw, I headed down the hall, one hand on the bassinette, the other pressed over my now-leaking incision. I glanced into the hospital room again as I passed and had no doubts. Reid, pacing rapidly, was still on the phone.

"Jim, buddy, I just want to stop in and show you some of the key man plans we can offer."

I shoved Caitlin's bassinette, like a cartful of groceries, into my room, skidded in, and slammed the door. I pressed my incision with my palm, which seemed right now to be the only thing preventing my intestines from spilling out onto the floor. I peered over the bassinette's edge. Caitlin's eyelids were purplish white, patterned with tiny pink veins.

I had dreamed of running into Reid. In those dreams I was slim and svelte, happy and published. Jeff, stunningly handsome, successful, witty and attentive, was at my side. In my more enjoyable dreams, Reid was toothless, alone, and used a cane. He was always wearing the same awful red and gray argyle sweater.

I shuffled to the mirror. I still looked about four months pregnant. My stomach felt like semi-congealed Jello. My hair was thick from the pregnancy, but how careless of me to neglect washing and setting it during labor and delivery. I had on no make-up. My nightgown and robe didn't even match.

But wasn't too late. Caitlin was still asleep. I turned on the shower, and stripped down. Warm soothing water pummeled my aching sagging body. Why should I be surprised to run into Reid in the hospital? After all, Reid was always in the hospital. For some reason, the moment Reid had said his vows, he had become an instant hypochondriac. The high-energy marketing major I'd married transformed overnight into a guy who would do almost anything to get admitted to whatever ward could squeeze him in. Double rooms were better because they provided built-in conversation victims, most of whom were in no shape to run out of the room. Once installed in a narrow bed with its matching narrow closet, Reid would put a shapeless argyle sweater over his cotton gown and pad around the corridors discussing his ailments with anybody he happened to meet.

The last time had been five years ago when Reid had been hospitalized for a slipped disc. I had practically lived at the hospital, eating alone in the cafeteria, smoking in the courtyard, sitting beside Reid for hours, separated by only a white curtain from an enormous pale man who constantly tried to clear phlegm from his throat. That time, after Reid came home, during a short window of time in which he seemed healthy, I had left.

Now, thinking about Reid and his family two doors down, I felt my jaw involuntarily tighten. Not only had Reid taken our only good car, and the oriental rug my aunt had given us as a wedding gift, he was now keeping me prisoner in my hospital room with the door closed. And Jeff wasn't even here, whereas obviously Reid's new wife, having just given birth, was. He was definitely ahead. If you were keeping score. And, I realized, I was.

Smiling grimly, I rubbed blush on the taut muscles of my cheeks

I had, with idiotic first-time mother optimism, brought a pair of pre-pregnancy black corduroys with me. The day after Caitlin was born I'd examined the waistband with hilarity and disbelief. Now I yanked them from my suitcase and tossed them onto the bed like a gauntlet, like a flag before a bull. Dammit, I was wearing those suckers. Just watch me.

I managed to pull the waistband up and over my rear end but with my leaking incision pulling up the zipper was out of the question. Fortunately, my maternity sweater now came down to my knees. The phone rang.

"Honey?" Jeff sounded as though he'd just run a 10K. "I've been trying for over an hour. I can't get the car out."

I looked out the window. Sparkling flakes swirled in a feverish dance. "Oh, please, Jeff, you can't leave me here!"

"What's wrong? Is something wrong with Caitlin?"

I glanced at the baby. "What? No, no, she's fine, but this hospital is driving me crazy, I have to get out of here."

"Well, it's probably not even a good idea to transport the baby in this kind of weather."

I looked out the window at the glaring white. "Oh." A day by myself in the hospital hiding from Reid and his lovely wife, two doors down. I heaved what I knew was a very melodramatic and manipulative sigh. As usual, Jeff was being sensible.

"They're calling this the blizzard of the century. I'll keep trying, but it doesn't look good."

Just as we hung up, Sandy, the nurse, bustled in. She plumped my pillows with karate chops. "Ready to try breast-feeding again?"

"OK." I picked up the baby, as if she were porcelain, and glided, trying not to wake her, toward the bed. Sandy, with a disapproving glare, took Caitlin, dumped her on the bed, then unwrapped Caitlin's blanket and began to thump the bottoms of her feet.

"If she doesn't wake up to eat every four hours, you need to wake her up. Why don't you get in bed." It wasn't a question.

I complied.

"You need to time each side." Sandy twisted Caitlin's head and shoved it into my breast as if she were handing off a football. Her hands looked red and worn, and she had no-nonsense lines around her mouth. "She's not made of glass."

"Uh-huh." This situation with Reid was so awkward. Surely the adult thing to do would be to congratulate him. Hiding out like this was ridiculous.

"You need to drink plenty of fluids." Sandy slid a tray with a cup of light green liquid within reach. "Otherwise you won't have enough milk. By the way, how's your incision? Let's take a look."

If Sandy saw it leaking she might not let me go home.

"It's fine, I just checked it."

Sandy narrowed her eyes, hesitated, then hurried out.

Breast-feeding made me feel relaxed and sleepy. Caitlin had the most intoxicating smell. Just stroking her miraculously smooth and flawless cheek gave me the most exquisite feeling of well-being. I looked at the clock beside the TV and made a mental note to switch Caitlin to the other breast in ten minutes.

An hour or so later, I awoke with Caitlin fast asleep at my drained right breast while the left was so turgid it had begun to leak through my sweater. So had my incision. Painfully hoisting myself out of bed, I returned Caitlin to her bassinette.

I saw that Sandy had left the door open and crossed the room to close it.

At that moment Reid stepped into the hall.

Our eyes met for one of those fleeting instants before instinctive social graces kick in. Reid's face registered shock and embarrassment.

"Hi!" we both instantly stretched smiles across our faces.

"I heard from the Clarks that you were pregnant—" Reid gestured awkwardly at my abdomen.

"I thought I saw you this morning—"

We'd spoken simultaneously and now we both fell silent. Reid was thinner and less intimidating than I remembered.

"This is such an amazing coincidence." I smoothed my sweater to make sure it covered my unzipped pants. Maybe he wouldn't notice the large yellow stain clinging to my left breast at the top of the sweater and the smaller pink one bunched down below. "I have a baby girl. What about you?"

"A boy," Reid said. "He sure is something. Laura's feeding him now. Listen, why don't I bring them over? Laura would love to meet you."

How very civilized. Behind me, in the room, the baby fussed a little. Warm colostrum spurted out of my swollen left breast.

"Sounds perfect," I said. "Give me about ten minutes, okay?"

I skidded into the bathroom and tried to pump my milk into a baby bottle. I gave up after spraying milk on the mirror, the wall, the toilet, and into my own eye. There seemed to be no way of telling which way the milk was going. Finally I squirted it into the sink. I knew the nurse would yell at me, but Caitlin was deeply asleep and what the hell else was I going to do? I'd just finished stuffing a folded piece of toilet paper over the soaked incision bandage when my visitors arrived.

"Hi." Laura, pushing her baby's bassinette, had blonde, curly hair, jingly silver earrings, and wore a man's plaid robe. She looked a little like Reid's mother might have looked a few decades ago. "What a coincidence, hey? I've always wanted to meet you. I bet you and Reid set this up." She laughed.

"Come on in," I said. "What's his name?" The baby's face was still red and, to me, he looked and smelled very unappealing.

"Reid Junior," Reid boomed. "What else?" I had forgotten how loud Reid's voice was.

"Isn't he a pistol? Let's take a look at your little stinker." Reid and Laura peered over the edge of the bassinette as Caitlin slept.

"How sweet," said Laura.

I gazed with awe at the curve of Caitlin's lashes as they brushed her cheeks, her flawless skin, and the downy hair on the nape of her neck. Her aroma was an absolute aphrodisiac. She was not, excuse me, a stinker.

"How much weight did you gain?" Laura settled herself beside Reid on my bed.

Rather a personal question, I thought, for someone I'd known for less than five minutes. I lowered myself into the nursing chair and shifted my weight to one thigh. With both a C-section and an episiotomy, nearly any position was a challenge.

"Laura gained twenty pounds exactly, and she's already lost all but three pounds," Reid shouted before I could answer. "Doesn't she look great?"

"Oh, yes." So he was keeping score too.

"We went all natural," Laura announced. "How about you?"

"Oh, the cord was around Caitlin's neck so I had to have a C-section."

"Too bad."

Two points to the plaid team.

"Well, at least her head doesn't look smushed," I said, wincing at my own audacity. Two for the unzipped corduroy team.

Sandy popped in and with rapid sleight of hand replaced my empty juice cup with a full one and placed a little paper cup containing a pain pill on my tray.

"Laura's labor was eighteen hours and she never took a thing. A couple of times she was begging for it but she made me promise not to let her have anything so I didn't." Reid squeezed his wife's shoulder with exaggerated affection.

Three pointer.

"Did you know we videotaped Reid Junior's birth?" Laura said.

"I was right down there with the camera in close-up living color," Reid chimed in. "Even when Laura was in transition and she was screaming her fool head off."

"Goodness," I said, having completely lost track of the score.

"Listen," said Reid suddenly. "I hold no grudge whatsoever, do you, Lisa?"

Well, except for the car, Aunt Katherine's oriental rug, and four years of my life. But I smiled. "Of course not."

"Everything was for the best," Reid boomed, squeezing his wife's shoulder again. "Although I want you to know, Lisa, that I did have to go back to the hospital and get my back operated on after all, and recuperation was no picnic."

Laura rolled her eyes. I smiled and nodded, feeling a sudden affection for her.

"I see you're still wearing that lovely argyle sweater," I said to Reid. Briefly, remembering him plodding down the hospital halls in this shapeless sweater, a lump formed in my throat. I knew, now, why he kept getting sick while we were married, and I was glad he'd found someone to love him.

I wish Jeff had walked in at just that moment, his black hair sparkling with melting snow, his cheeks beet red from the cold, having hailed a passing snowplow. Maybe Jeff would have proved himself to be much the better match for me, and Reid would have shown himself to be happy with Laura. And Jeff would have braved the elements to take me home from the hospital just the way I wanted.

But instead, Laura said "Maybe we'll run into each other in nursery school orientation," then pushed her baby's bassinette out the door. As she passed, I looked down at the baby again. His eyes moved back and forth under his closed, translucent lids, and I wondered what he was watching in there, and decided he seemed quite lovable after all. Then Reid and his family were gone.

Jeff didn't make it to get Caitlin and me until the next day. It turned out that my brother-in-law was also stuck in the hospital, as the snow had hit while he was visiting his father, who was very ill, and he stopped by and took some videos of Caitlin that are nothing less than priceless. He took one particular shot of me holding her close where I'm puckering up trying to kiss her and she is imitating me, squinting and puckering, too. We both have the most unbelievably chapped lips; we look as though we've been through hell together, and in a way, we have. Our lips are so chapped we look as though we'd slice each other open with the slightest kiss.

You wouldn't believe the coincidence," I said to Jeff when he finally arrived. "My ex-husband Reid and his wife Laura are two doors down. She just had a little boy. Do you " want to meet them?"

"No," said Jeff, who has always avoided small talk. He wasn't the least bit jealous of my ex-husband and had no desire to visit the past. He has always looked forward. "We need to get out of here. It's supposed to start snowing again. Ready?"

"Yes! We just need to put on Caitlin's snowsuit."

Her bowed spindly legs reached only an inch or so below the crotch, leaving the entire lower section of the snowsuit dangling empty. Her little hands barely reached the suit's armpits. Jeff leaned over her, his face fatigued, but with an expression of such tenderness that my eyes stung and my throat felt tight.

Sandy, pushing a wheelchair, patted the seat, indicating I was to sit down. "Hospital rules." I sat. "Now, Dad, why don't you let Mom carry the baby."

Jeff was Dad. I was Mom. Jeff reverently laid Caitlin in my lap.

Sandy bent to rearrange Caitlin's blankets, her red, lined hands in sharp contrast to the baby's ivory skin. I slid my finger under Caitlin's tiny hand and with a pure and magical reflex, Caitlin's fingers circled mine. The trusting way she slept, as I held her, told me that the games were over. This was a whole new world.

THIS IS FOR JANET

Calvin Quinn drove his dented blue Volkswagen Beetle past the tobacco factory, past Mount Zion Baptist Church, and past the coliseum where he had only last week received his high school diploma. He was listening to Casey Kasem's American Top 40 countdown on the radio.

"It had to be kismet," Kasem said now. "Raoul was parking cars in an underground garage by day and playing in a band by night. One day he parked the Jaguar of top record producer Michael Zucconi and he took a chance. He put a tape from his own band in Mr. Zucconi's tape player and made sure it was playing when he delivered the car. The rest is history."

Calvin loved the way Kasem made success sound mythical, inevitable. He began creating a Kasem story for himself. "Few names in rock-n-roll history have transcended the title of disc jockey. Wolfman Jack. Don Imus. Dick Clark. Now we add another name to the list of legends of the airwaves...Calvin Quinn." He spotted WRAR's radio tower in the distance. To his surprise, he did not feel nervous. He felt like part of a Casey Kasem countdown, part of history.

Nestled in his shirt pocket was a tape he had painstakingly labeled "Calvin Quinn, Audition Tape, May 1973," just the way they said to do it in *Billboard* magazine. This he had recorded in his own bedroom while staring at a poster of Led Zeppelin in the light of a lava lamp. He had seen vocalists hold microphones so close they brushed their lips. He did that too.

When Calvin listened to his voice on tape, it sounded completely different from the rest of him, deep and rich, like something he should share with people. Calvin loved the idea of his voice racing through the air at the speed of light and finding its way to people's ears while they were sitting in their cars, lying by the pool, fixing lunch, or doing heart surgery. He loved the way a disc jockey could make you feel as though you belonged to a secret club, like a cool friend who otherwise would never like you.

When Calvin looked in the mirror, he saw a small, pale, fearful person. His voice, he believed, was the representation of his true self, an inner self who was righteous, courageous, and destined for success.

Calvin pulled his VW bug into a parking space marked "Visitor" in front of the station. He'd expected a handsome high-rise building with King-Kong-sized call letters. In reality, WRAR was a one-story structure covered with light green aluminum siding. He knew he was in the right place, because the call letters were painted on the glass front door. Admittedly, they slanted slightly downhill.

Coming out of that glass door was a person whose face he knew from a billboard—Rufus Washington, WRAR's longtime graveyard jock, who opened his show each night with a signature howl at the moon. Rufus Washington was a thin man with coffee-colored skin. He still wore Afro Sheen on his hair, even though decades ago every other black person in America had stopped. Calvin, who liked noticing details about celebrities, saw that Washington was smoking a Camel nonfilter. Calvin didn't dare say hello, but saw it as providential that he had crossed paths with Washington on the way to his interview, and he felt a shiver of delight when Washington nodded and grunted, "Mornin'." Calvin made a mental note to start smoking Camel nonfilters.

Larry "Hands" Pagano, station manager for WRAR, was a former Atlantic Coast Conference basketball star. Calvin later learned that Pagano had fallen into the radio business knowing nothing about it but had quickly learned one lesson that had served him well: some people love this so much they will do it for free.

Now Calvin held his breath as he watched one of those huge, famed hands, heavy with an ACC championship ring, press PLAY on the tape deck, and then heard his own voice fill Pagano's expansive, thick-carpeted office.

"Hey, it's a beautiful night, and I wish I were sitting in my car down by the quarry with Janet. We'd talk a little bit about stuff that happened today, like the fight in the cafeteria, or the argument that Janet had with her mom, or how the guy at 7-Eleven wouldn't sell us cigarettes. And then I'd slide a tape into the tape deck and play this song. Janet, this is for you. " Next Calvin had laid down the opening riffs to "Stairway to Heaven."

"Well," said Mr. Pagano, tossing Calvin's audition tape back to him, "You've got a good voice. I like the way you work the girlfriend into your routine." When he stood up behind his desk, his head almost popped one of the ceiling tiles.

"Somebody the other day was telling me we need a traffic reporter. You know, for morning and afternoon drive time. I'd like you to give that a shot, on a volunteer basis, for three months or so. If things work out, you can jump right on board."

Calvin slid the tape back into his pocket, firm against his chest. He breathed a sigh of joy. He had heard the words "on board." A few seconds later he realized what the station manager wanted him to do had nothing to do with music. Or money.

Lisa Williams Kline

"Traffic," he said.

"That's right."

"Uh, OK."

"Welcome to the team, Big Guy." Mr Pagano leaned over his desk and crushed Calvin's hand in his. Kismet. Just the way Casey Kasem had described it. Well, almost.

People called in to tell Calvin about the traffic in their area. Calvin, who hardly had courage to speak to people when they were standing in the same room, found himself joking around with faceless callers and achieving levels of intimacy he'd never known face to face. Soon he had a regular group of commuters from around the city who called each hour to talk about the traffic on the major arteries. He opened his traffic report with fifteen seconds of "Crosstown Traffic" by Hendrix. Then he started his routine.

"Hey, this is Calvin Quinn, and it looks brutal out there tonight. There's stop-and-go traffic on I-40 downtown and about a twenty minute backup on Route 52. Janet left work about five minutes ago to come over to my place, and it's my guess she's stuck on Silas Creek Parkway. Janet, whoever gets there first starts the bubble bath."

He ended his report with "Baby You Can Drive My Car" by the Beatles.

Calvin became slowly aware that people loved his voice. He was an invisible friend, a compatriot in arms against the brutalities, the indignities, the aggravation of rush-hour traffic.

The traffic report had to get a separate phone line, and the station hired people just to answer the phones. They would take notes and feed the information to Calvin in the control room. Local businesses were lining up to sponsor the traffic report, and Calvin started reading advertisements in between accidents and tie-ups.

Calvin loved sitting in the control room with an ashtray full of squashed Camel nonfilters, in a haze of smoke, sipping coffee and tweaking the audio, telling people how to get to work and home again.

"Why don't you ask for a raise, my man?" said Rufus Washington one gray dawn as he crossed paths with Calvin in the control room. Calvin was still in a state of awe that he and Washington had normal conversations, like two ordinary people. Calvin had by this time heard many legends about Rufus Washington, one of which was that several years ago, Rufus had put on "In-a-Gadda-Da-Vida" and done the dirty deed with a lady friend in the lobby and was back at the microphone five seconds before the song came to an end.

Calvin didn't know whether that was true or not. All he knew was that Rufus had a record collection of 45s and even 78s that was a quarter of a century old. Calvin would sit with Rufus and watch him clean his records, his long fingers resting gently on the edges, sliding a velvet cylinder in a measured wagon wheel motion. Rufus was always getting in trouble with Mr. Pagano for playing blues and jazz instead of Top 40 tunes.

"A raise?" Calvin repeated now. "But I'm only a volunteer."

Rufus clapped him on the shoulder with a phlegmy half-cough, half-laugh. "You have any idea how many spots the Handsman has sold because of your traffic report? You go in there and ask for you a salary."

So Calvin finally started getting paid.

He was like morning coffee, like the orange juice and cereal people ate for breakfast. He could feel them all out there, searching for the comfort of his voice, listening for him to tell them which way to go. He loved them, each and every one of them; he loved them all.

"Hey, this is Calvin Quinn. Listen up everybody. A truckload of musical instruments has overturned at the intersection of Stratford Road and I-40. This is no lie, folks. One of my callers said there are tubas and ukeleles scattered across two lanes. Janet, take the back roads, baby."

Then one day Mr. Pagano called him into his office. There was a broad-shouldered guy with wavy brown hair sitting in front of Mr. Pagano's desk, a guy with a wide grin and a beefy handshake.

"Calvin," said Mr. Pagano. "This is Alan Young. He's our new helicopter pilot."

Less than a week later Calvin was numbly strapping himself in beside Alan in the 5:30 A.M. chill, listening to the deafening beat of the propellers. He put on his headset.

"Hi, it's Calvin Quinn," he shouted, "and we're broadcasting live from our helicopter for the very first time this morning. Janet, this is fantastic. I could fly over the Reynolda Road backup right now and probably look down and see you sitting in the car on your way to work, using the mirror on the visor to put on your makeup. Alan is here with me; he's our friendly pilot."

"Hi, Janet," said Alan, winking at Calvin.

Calvin had begun to get invitations to receptions, premieres, political hooplas, and the occasional orgy. One day Alan, hanging around Calvin's desk, shuffled through several of the heavy creamy envelopes with black spidery writing on the outside.

"Wow," Alan said. "Looks like you're booked solid this weekend."

"I never go to any of these things."

"You're kidding! Do you have any idea how much free food and how many gorgeous babes you're passing up?" Alan hesitated. "Or you could, you know, take Janet."

"You go if you want. Here." Calvin thrust the sheaf of unopened invitations at Alan.

The pilot narrowed his eyes. "Why don't you go to any of these things?"

Calvin held the invitations out to him. "You go."

So on Monday mornings now, while they were taking off from the station's new helipad, Alan would tell Calvin about all the fun he had missed that weekend.

"OK, that one on the silver paper with the blue writing, that was at the new art museum. Calvin, they had these two tables with standing rib roasts and these guys in tall white hats, and they said, 'How do you like yours, sir?' They also had caviar and shrimp as big as my ear, and these guys in tuxedos were walking around with silver trays full of skinny champagne glasses. It was primo, buddy."

"Do women like me, Alan?"

Alan looked over at him and grinned. He held up his thumb. "Definitely."

They were three stories up, and the wind was soaring around them, cold and loud. Calvin looked at his watch and put on his headset.

A new employee showed up beside Calvin's desk one day. She was tall and thin with waist-length red hair that looked as if she'd stuck her finger in an electrical socket. Her skin was pale and freckled, and her eyelashes were so light, her eyes looked naked.

"Is this the traffic department?" she said.

"Uh no," said Calvin. "This is where we do the traffic report. The traffic department where they do the production log is just around the corner. I guess that's kind of confusing."

She flipped her hair behind her shoulder. "You must know Calvin Quinn, the traffic reporter," she said.

"Yeah, sure," he said.

"He's like my guru. I listen to him every day."

"I'll introduce you sometime."

"Cool. You know," she said, flipping her hair behind her shoulder again, "I'm really a writer. I'm going to write commercials. I may be stuck in traffic now but I'm going to move up."

"I admire that in a person," said Calvin.

"My name's Lucy," she said, holding out a freckled hand with long white fingers.

Calvin made an appointment with Mr. Pagano to talk about his future.

"I want to be a DJ when a spot opens up," he said.

"No can do," said the station manager. "The team needs you right where you are." He balled up a piece of paper and threw it across the room at a trash can. "Two!" he shouted as Calvin closed the office door.

"He's not going to give me a shot at it," Calvin told Rufus Washington that night. Calvin had run into Rufus at a downtown club where Muddy Waters was playing. Rufus, to Calvin's surprise, was alone and appeared to be drunk, so Calvin drove him home. Calvin had expected Rufus to live in a fancy hotel and was surprised to learn that he lived in a run-down apartment with weeds out front, peeling paint, and rusty, uneven Venetian blinds and spider webs in the front window. Rufus didn't invite Calvin in but brought the crate containing his record collection outside on the porch. They sat in graying wooden rocking chairs and talked music.

"Can I play this?" Calvin asked Rufus, holding up a new Herbie Hancock album called *Headhunters*.

"Nope, had to pawn my stereo. But I'll be getting it back in a coupla weeks, guaranteed." Rufus unsteadily held a lighter at the end of his Camel for some seconds before he managed to light it. He waved dismissively in Calvin's direction. "You go ahead; take it home."

"Wow. Thanks."

"Don't you let the old Handsman play his sly games with you, boy," Rufus said as Calvin made his way down the porch steps. "You make him pay you what you deserve."

"OK," said Calvin.

The next morning Calvin came in, chilled and windblown from morning rush hour, and Lucy was standing by his desk with her arms folded. Her lashless blue eyes were narrowed. "You ARE Calvin Quinn," she accused him.

"Who told you that?" Calvin started looking through his mail. He dumped a three-inch stack of invitations in the trash can. Lucy didn't go away.

"Mr. Pagano told me. Why did you pretend not to be yourself/"

"I guess I like my privacy," Calvin said, immediately regretting it.

"Well, excuse me for prying."

Calvin watched her hair fly around her elbow like children around a maypole as she turned to go. "Wait," he said. He wet his lips. "I'm sorry."

Lucy slipped one thigh over the edge of his desk. "I've applied for a job as a copywriter. They want a tape. Your voice is perfect for my writing." She handed him a piece of paper that had been folded several times into a thick multilayered square, then she disappeared down the hall, the red tendrils of her hair swaying in the small of her back.

Calvin put the paper in his pocket, where it throbbed with heat and emanated musky perfume.

"OK, everybody, this is Calvin Quinn, and traffic's moving along pretty well today. Janet, this may be the last few minutes you're able to get our broadcast signal. Janet is just heading out, traveling cross-country in a Jeep, taking pictures of Americans from sea to shining sea. I'm going to miss you, baby, see you in three months!"

Calvin removed his headset and looked at the tiny cars below, glinting and snaking along the highways like slow-moving insects. He realized he had lied to his people. There was an accident on Cherry Street, and rush hour wasn't going to move smoothly at all; it was going to be a nightmare.

"Three months?" Alan shouted.

Calvin nodded.

About a week later, Mr. Pagano buzzed Calvin in the booth while he was recording Lucy's ad copy.

"Calvin, we're getting a lot of feedback about, you know, uh, Janet."

"Oh, really?"

"Seems like a lot of your listeners miss her. Hasn't she been in touch with you?"

"Sure, yeah, she calls, writes postcards, the usual."

"How about reading a postcard on the air or something? Let the people know what she's doing."

"OK, no problem."

"By the way," Mr. Pagano went on. "Where is she now?"

"Uh...St. Louis, I think."

"H'mmm." Mr. Pagano's voice dropped. "That sounds pretty dull."

Calvin hesitated. "Well, she's going rafting down the Rio Grande in a few days."

"Better."

"And she's planning to go to Las Vegas, I think."

"That's the ticket, Big Guy. Super. Let's build the tension until she gets back." Mr. Pagano waited a beat. "She is coming back?"

"I don't know."

The next day, between an accident and a disabled vehicle, Calvin sandwiched in a short postcard from Janet in St. Louis. A few days later he read a letter from Janet describing the Grand Canyon. The letter contained descriptions of people Janet was photographing in her travels, from the smooth faces of infants to the grizzled faces of old-timers, to a Cherokee woman with hatchet like cheekbones and black hair to her waist.

Meanwhile, one morning Calvin invited Lucy to the Krispy Kreme right down the block from the station. He asked for a table where they could watch the doughnut production line. He especially liked the way the lines of doughnuts, one after another, got dunked in sugar glaze and came up streaming and shiny.

"Thanks for recording the spot for me," Lucy said, picking up her doughnut in her white, freckled fingers. Calvin watched her break the doughnut in half and then lick the sugar off her pink, oval fingertips.

"My pleasure," he said.

"I'm sick of this slow-motion Southern town," she said. "I'm going to become a big-time New York copywriter. I have this vision of myself on Madison Avenue in funky business suits and fuchsia high heels."

"What if things between Janet and me don't, you know, work out?" Calvin said slowly, clearing his throat.

Lucy hunched over her plate and squinted at him. "What do you mean? Sounds to me like you and Janet have the perfect relationship. I mean, that letter from the Grand Canyon was sheer poetry." She ate another section of doughnut.

And then Calvin blurted it out. "Do I look the way you expected me to?"

The white skin on her cheeks turned pinkish. She looked down and picked at something under her index fingernail. "Calvin," she said finally, "people on the radio never look the way you expect them to." Then she smiled. Her teeth were small and shiny. "You know I love your voice." She looked at her watch. "Listen, I've got to get going. Thanks for the tape. I sent it over to this guy and I'm waiting for him to call. Alan promised to fly me over if the guy wants to see me right away." She patted his arm. "You're very sweet," she said.

She hurried out. Calvin stayed and finished his doughnut, studying the smudged pink rim Lucy's lipstick had left on her coffee cup.

That evening, as Calvin switched on the mike for his rush-hour traffic report, Alan veered the copter in a last broad loop to head home. The sun sank low and orange, and the bumper-to-bumper traffic below began to look like a double-stranded glow-in-the-dark necklace.

Lisa Williams Kline

"There's a fender bender about a mile north of the Stratford Road overpass that has turned the usual slow-moving rush hour traffic into a gridlock nightmare. Rubbernecking is making it even worse. Expect delays getting out of the city on 52, I-40, and Reynolda Road. I got a letter from Janet today, a portion of which I'd like to read."

When Alan looked at Calvin, the pilot's face was pale in the fading light.

"Dear Calvin. I'm out West now. It's vast and deserted, and the air smites your nostrils, and you can wait all day for a single car to go by. There is no traffic here, Calvin. People go wherever they want at whatever speed they choose. I'm staying here. Will you come stay here, too?"

Alan's eyes widened, and his mouth dropped open.

"Love, Janet," Calvin finished. He took a deep breath. "And that's Calvin's Quinn's traffic report for WRAR radio."

Calvin could hear the tinny prerecorded "Expressway to Your Heart" over his headset as he removed it.

"How can a traffic reporter go somewhere that has no traffic?" Alan screamed at him over the propeller roar. They flew on through the cold, throbbing night. A full orange moon loomed on the horizon.

"You're not actually going to go, are you?" Then Alan laughed and poked his elbow at Calvin. "Can I have your job? Dozens of women already think I'm you, anyway."

Calvin didn't answer.

That very night Rufus Washington locked himself in the control room at 2:00 A.M., ripped out the phone, and started playing the blues. He skipped the Top 40 tunes; he skipped the commercials. He played Miles Davis; he played B.B. King. He played "The Thrill is Gone" seventeen times in a row.

When Calvin got to work at five, he saw Mr. Pagano standing in the hallway outside the control room while a uniformed security guard used a crowbar on the locked door.

The door swung open. B.B. King's cracked voice rushed out. Rufus swung around in a cloud of cigarette smoke and saw the uniform.

"Are you trying to arrest me for playing the blues?"

"This is a Top 40 radio station," said Mr. Pagano. "Not blues. Not jazz. And you're fired."

Rufus, as he was being escorted out the front door by the security guard, flicked a burning Camel nonfilter onto the carpet. He looked back at Calvin once and pointed a long, gray finger.

"Don't forget what I told you about the sly games," was all he said.

"OK, Big Guy," Mr. Pagano said to Calvin. "Rufus has fouled out of the game. I need a graveyard jock." The record ended and Calvin stood beside Mr. Pagano and listened to the rhythmic *scratch, scratch* as the needle went round and round in the same spot.

Here was the golden opportunity that Casey Kasem always talked about. That magic moment when what you've always wanted crashes into kismet. It didn't feel the way Calvin thought it would. Casey Kasem never said that everyone's beginning is an end for someone else.

"We'll get your promotional shots done and send out a press release later this morning," Mr. Pagano was saying. "Remember the drill: Play a Top 40 hit, an oldie, then go to commercial. Got that? Top 40 hit, oldie, go to commercial."

Calvin saw a reflection of himself in the control room window. His narrow, sloped shoulders, thin ratlike face, his mop of black hair.

"And another thing," Mr. Pagano was saying. "Today we'll start a one-week countdown, and I want you to bring Janet back at midnight next Saturday night. For a ....steamy reunion." Mr. Pagano slapped Calvin on the back. "Knock yourself out, Big Guy."

Calvin took a deep breath. Then he stepped into the booth and put on the headset, still warm and smelling like Afro Sheen.

Someone handed him a cup of coffee. He lit a cigarette and cued up "Stairway to Heaven." Resting his fingertips lightly on the pots, he pulled the mike so close, his lips gently brushed its nubby surface. "This is for Janet," he said.

WEBS

Parker sat on the stool, her hands folded in her lap. A stray hair poked at the edge of her eye. She blew upwards gently but could not dislodge the hair. Her eye started to water.

Quickly, she unfolded her hands, and wiped the hair from her eye.

"Miss Parker! Haven't I told you not to move your hands?"

"Yes, ma'am."

Now Parker had an itch between her shoulder blades. Once she'd seen a bear at the Asheboro Zoo scratching his back against a tree trunk, and she'd like to do that right now. She looked with longing out the tall window of Miss Annabelle's studio. The leaves on the big oak tree in the back yard waved gaily like the hands of all the other third graders who did not have to sit for their portraits this summer and who were instead sleeping late, riding skateboards in the carports, and swimming in the warm muddy creeks.

Miss Annabelle liked early morning light best. Parker could still see the glitter of dew on a spider web in the corner of the window. Far beyond the spider web she saw Roland Gant climbing out of a second story window of the Ramsay's house. She watched him crabwalk across the porch roof, shimmy down a corner pole, and run into the woods.

Roland was a black guy in high school whom everyone knew because he had blue eyes. His skin was light brown and looked soft as suede. One time at church Parker heard a man say if we went to school with negras first thing you know there would be a bunch of brown babies with blue eyes. Roland's eyes were the palest ice blue, and they made him look a little bit crazy. Mark Taylor, a sixth-grader who rode Parker's school bus, said Roland **was** crazy. Parker wondered what he was doing on the second floor of the Ramsay's house.

Mary Ellen Ramsay had babysat for Parker and her brother a few weeks ago. She had used the fancy ash tray in the living room that you weren't really supposed to use to smoke some skinny lumpy cigarettes. Mary Ellen ignored Parker and her brother Ben, and wasn't even interested when Parker told her the story about being born on the day President Kennedy was shot and her mother thinking her baby had been stolen because the nurses were watching television and didn't bring her.

Mary Ellen Ramsay hadn't babysat for them again. It must have been because of the ash tray because Parker didn't tell her parents anything.

"Miss Parker! Please turn your head this way."

"Yes, ma'm."

Parker could not see Miss Annabelle. She could see the back of the easel and Miss Annabelle's shoes. The soles were rubbery and squeaked when Miss Annabelle crossed the room to get a new brush or tube of paint. Miss Annabelle lit long, thin cigarettes which she placed in the ashtray and forgot about, leaving fragile snaking cylinders of ash which collapsed if you touched them. Miss Annabelle had lots of paint brushes sitting around in empty coffee cans. During one sitting Parker lost count at 150.

The tubes of paint had beautiful names. Alizarin crimson. Cerulean blue. Raw umber. Miss Annabelle swirled pristine globs of colors together with rapid brush movements or by scraping with a tool that looked like a tiny garden spade. Sometimes Parker looked at something and tried to imagine how Miss Annabelle would reproduce its color. Roland Gant's skin, for instance. Burnt sienna and titanium white.

"All right, we're all finished for today." Miss Annabelle put down her brush and, with a swift movement, covered the portrait with a sheet.

Parker's right leg was asleep and the undersides of her thighs were wet with sweat. Pretending to stomp on her foot to get the blood back into it, she tilted her head to try to glimpse what Miss Annabelle had painted so far.

Miss Annabelle placed herself between Parker and the portrait.

"I don't allow peeking, young lady."

Miss Annabelle had an old face, long, skinny, and almost as wrinkled as Parker's grandmother's. Parker's mother described her hair as "so <u>very</u> red" and then would look at Parker's father with a little smile. Miss Annabelle's hair made Parker feel cheerful. But it wasn't really red. It was orange, a color you would get if you combined cadmium red light with cadmium yellow light.

In the bathroom Parker took off the white gloves, the white patent leather shoes, the lacy white socks, and the peach organdy dress.

"The dress please!" Miss Annabelle's voice came from outside the bathroom door before Parker had time to drop the dress on the floor. Goose-bumpy in her undershirt, she cracked the door, and handed out the dress.

Then she stepped into her overalls and pulled her straw-colored hair into a ponytail. Miss Annabelle made her wear her hair down because she said ponytails don't look good in portraits. Parker folded the white socks into a tight ball. She'd ridden her skateboard over here barefoot every day and now the socks were pretty dirty. Hopefully Miss Annabelle wouldn't notice.

"Bye, Miss Annabelle. See you tomorrow," she called into the studio. Miss Annabelle never answered her. All Parker saw were Miss Annabelle's shoes and a curl of smoke coming from behind the easel.

Usually by the time Parker got down the porch steps and into the sunshine she broke into a skip, and the anguish of the previous hour vanished into the blue sky like a lost balloon. She'd skip down the sidewalk between Miss Annabelle's purple-blue hydrangea bushes, jump at the last crack, land on her skateboard, and fly down the street towards home.

Roland Gant crossed the street a block ahead of her. He was walking briskly, with a kind of syncopation to his walk, not with the slow, purposeful movements of the yardmen and gardeners in the neighborhood. Parker touched a bare foot to the pavement to slow her skateboard and then skated two lazy circles in the road to make sure he got across before she got there. She wasn't afraid of Roland, exactly. Once or twice in the past she'd been close enough for him to notice her, and, although he never had, she'd felt a tightening of excitement that she didn't understand. It seemed that if he turned his ice-blue gaze on her she might freeze. Or melt. She wasn't sure.

As soon as he disappeared past the corner Parker pushed her bare foot three quick times on the pavement and headed home. Last year Mark Taylor, at the end of the summer, had stuck a needle in the bottom of his foot to prove to all the kids in the neighborhood how tough his feet were after three whole months barefoot. This summer that was Parker's goal.

"This other girl I know, Betsy Critchfield, had her portrait painted, but she didn't have to sit for it. The artist just took her picture and came back a few weeks later and voila! there was her portrait."

Parker tried to talk without moving her lips and studied Miss Annabelle's shoes and ash tray for some reaction. She wondered if Miss Annabelle had noticed her natural use of the word "voila."

Miss Annabelle didn't answer for such a long time that Parker looked out the window to see if the spider web was still there from the day before. It was, and the spider was carefully wrapping up a dead fly. This was sickening to watch but Parker couldn't take her eyes away.

Then she saw Roland Gant crawl out of the second floor window of the Ramsay's house again. After he shimmied down the corner post of the porch someone leaned out of the window and threw something at him. Both people were laughing. The thing was his shirt and the person, Parker realized, after Roland had melted into the woods, was Mary Ellen Ramsay.

When Mary Ellen babysat for Parker and Ben she had worn a shirt that she said was from India and Parker could see the dark circles of her nipples through the thin cotton. When Mary Ellen moved her breasts swayed. Parker's mother's breasts never did that. Mary Ellen brought a record album with pictures of people sitting on blankets having a gigantic picnic and some of the people weren't wearing clothes. Mary Ellen played the album on their parents' stereo without asking, and sang along with all the songs. One singer said he was "scared shitless, man," which was a word which had never been uttered in Parker's house ever.

"I will not paint a portrait from a photograph."

Parker was startled when Miss Annabelle finally responded to her comment and at first didn't remember what the conversation was about.

"I paint people, not photographs."

"Oh." Parker nodded her head as if to say "I see," although she didn't.

"These new business-oriented artists paint from photographs to save time. But they're painting a picture of a photograph. Not capturing the essence of the subject's soul."

"The essence?"

"As you sit here, day after day, we get to know each other. I paint, not only what I see, but what I learn about you as a person. The real you shows through."

Parker wondered how her real self could show through with this gauzy dress and gloves and lacy socks when she never wore stuff like that in real life but didn't say anything.

"If someone paints you from a photograph it's not only one-dimensional, it's an image of you at only one moment in time."

It occurred to Parker that she had now seen Roland Gant at two moments in time, maybe moments in time when nobody else saw him. And then there was also the time at her house, when Mary Ellen Ramsay babysat.

"Hundreds of years ago it was important for painters to paint realistically because there were no cameras to show us what people looked like. Now the purpose of portrait-painting has changed. People say the camera never lies. Well, when I paint, I can lie. Or I can tell more of the truth than a camera, if I want to."

Miss Annabelle peeked out from behind her canvas and her skinny face broke wide in a grin.

Parker grinned back, and swung her feet back and forth. "So, what do you do mostly, tell lies or tell the truth?"

"Oh, depends on my mood, I suppose." Miss Annabelle opened a fresh bottle of linseed oil and the smell floated towards Parker. "Once I did a portrait of two children. The children were both handsome to look at but I saw them treating others with cruelty and a lack of respect. So I told the truth and painted them ugly."

"Was their mother mad when she saw the portrait?" Parker's mother would be mad, she was sure of it.

"Oh, no. I do it in such a way that most people can't tell. It's my way of keeping a secret and telling the truth at the same time."

Parker thought about it. "How do you find out the truth about a person?"

Miss Annabelle's copper hair flashed from behind the canvas again.

"I get a sign. Sometimes I will look at a person for a week, just pretending to paint, because I haven't gotten any sign yet."

"Do you know the truth about me?" Parker had a flash of anxiety that the canvas in front of Miss Annabelle was blank.

"Well, I got closer to it today, I do believe." Miss Annabelle put down her brush and pulled the sheet over the canvas.

Parker skated a series of slow s-curves in the street on the way home, hoping to see Roland Gant again, maybe closer this time. But he had disappeared. Parker thought about "the truth." She thought of it as a hazy, amorphous blob, never quite in focus, sort of like the amoeba she'd seen under the microscope in school. She thought about it in relation to simple things, such as why her mother made her write a thank-you note telling Aunt Deborah how much she liked the grosgrain hair ribbons when she didn't. She also thought about it in relation to more complicated questions, such as why Aunt Deborah had never gotten married. (Her mother said it was just because she never met the right man.) And why President Kennedy had gotten shot. And why people would go on picnics naked. And why Roland Gant was sleeping over in Mary Ellen Ramsay's bedroom.

She longed to see what truth, if any, Miss Annabelle had seen in her face. Maybe if she could see what Miss Annabelle thought it would help her form her own opinion.

As she turned up her driveway, pushing her toughening foot against the hot pavement, she remembered how her parents often joked about the fact Miss Annabelle lived in a different century and never locked her doors.

The next morning when Parker woke up her pink alarm clock with tiny pricks of light around the perimeter said five-thirty. When she thought about what she was about to do, her heart began to pound so loudly she thought blood might spurt out her ears or at the very least her parents in the next room would hear it beating. The rustling of the sheets when she climbed out of bed sounded as loud as waves crashing on the beach. Miraculously, nobody heard.

She slipped into her overalls and tiptoed downstairs and wrote her mother a note which said, "Miss Annabelle wants me to come early." She decided against taking the skateboard, which would be too noisy.

Walking barefoot down her familiar street in the damp gray mist of early morning was spooky. The trees floating in half-light looked primitive, like trees from dinosaur times. The big front windows of Miss Annabelle's lopsided house looked like ghostly open eyes, and when a bird suddenly chirped in the stillness Parker almost jumped into one of Miss Annabelle's hydrangea bushes.

She'd decided to sneak around the back and go through the screened back porch. She could get in the studio, look at the portrait, and be out in only a minute or two.

Parker was trying to open the screen door without making it squeak when she heard a sharp firecracker sound. She collapsed behind a bush, letting the screen door slam, and looked in the direction of the sound.

Roland Gant was sliding head first down the Ramsay's back porch roof. He slid right off the end of the roof and fell to the ground and didn't move. Mary Ellen Ramsay was leaning out the window with something glinting black in her hand.

By the time Parker stopped running she was in her own backyard. She was shaking violently and there was a terrible roaring in her head. She thought again about the way Roland had slid like an old coat down the porch roof. A siren ripped through the morning stillness. She began to cry.

She tiptoed upstairs, trying to control her ragged breathing, and climbed into bed, clothes and all. She pulled the covers up to her neck. Realizing her feet were throbbing, she saw that they were bleeding from her run home. She wrapped tissues from the bedside table around her soles.

She lay in bed, her heart struggling inside her chest, and thought about what she had seen. In kindergarten at almost the end of the year a famous Negro minister had gotten shot and Parker had watched it on the news and noticed the scary limp way he fell, like Roland Gant. Roland Gant was sort of famous since everyone on the school bus was afraid of him. Roland Gant getting shot would not be on TV, though, because there weren't any people around. There was only Parker, who wasn't supposed to be there at all.

As the sun rose, morning light inched across the wall of her room. Parker was afraid to close her eyes so she was surprised when she opened them and her mother was sitting by her bed.

She sat up. "What time is it?"

"Don't worry, Miss Annabelle called, and you're not going to sit for your portrait today."

"Why?"

"Well, we thought you'd enjoy having a day off. You can go back tomorrow."

Parker searched her mother's face for secrets.

"Why did you wear your clothes to bed?" her mother asked.

Parker looked down at her overalls. Her thoughts were a jumble.

"I saw the note you wrote last night about needing to go to Miss Annabelle's early today," her mother went on. "Were you afraid you'd be late?"

Parker nodded. Her mother smiled and stroked her arm.

"Go back to sleep if you want to, honey."

Parker lay back down and her mother left the room. She wasn't sleepy even though the insides of her eyelids were burning from tiredness. Her body was rigid. She lay there without moving the whole morning, replaying in her mind what she had seen.

It had rained that night. The next day the spider web in Miss Annabelle's studio window had been washed away. Parker wondered if the spider had drowned. She could see yellow strips of plastic strung between the trees in the Ramsay's back yard which said "Do Not Cross." The strips looked like mimosa yellow, straight from the tube, not softened by white or black or any other color.

"You should have seen all the policemen yesterday," said Miss Annabelle. "Trampling my flowers and snooping around asking questions."

"What happened?" Parker thought her voice sounded strange and fakey when she said this, but Miss Annabelle didn't seem to notice.

"Oh, Lord, child, it was awful! A Negra crawled in Mary Ellen Ramsay's bedroom and tried to..." Miss Annabelle hesitated, and then said, "...rob her. She shot him."

Parker must have turned pale.

"Oh, honey, I'm sorry, maybe your mama didn't want you to know about it. I've always thought people lie to children too much. But I've scared you. It is awful. On our own street."

"He's dead?" Parker whispered. She thought about his blue eyes, water-washed like the sky, his velvet brown skin, his syncopated walk.

"Yes, it was just a terrible shame. They live just across the highway, you know, but it's a sure sign times are changing when they come over here into our neighborhoods and assault us and rob us."

Parker had never gotten a chance to touch his skin. It looked so warm and soft. The truth was, the color wasn't just burnt sienna and white, that was too simple; there would have to be just a pinch of carmine and cadmium yellow light. If you touched someone who was dead they would feel cold and maybe your finger would leave a dent, as if the skin had no will of its own and couldn't bounce back to its original shape.

"I can't paint a frown," Miss Annabelle was saying.

Parker tried to relax her face muscles.

"Will Mary Ellen have to go to jail?" she asked.

"Oh, I don't think so," said Miss Annabelle. "She will probably be let off on grounds of self-defense."

"Self-defense?"

"That means what she did is okay because she was defending herself from his attack."

Parker was silent. Parker couldn't sleep the night Mary Ellen babysat and while coming downstairs, she thought Roland Gant was attacking Mary Ellen because he pushed her up against the wall but she did not defend herself when he pushed her down on the couch and hunched on top of her. Mary Ellen told Roland he was a two-timer and Roland said no he wasn't in a smooth sugary voice, and then Roland Gant's hand slid under Mary Ellen's shirt from India in a way that made Parker's stomach flip. And then Mary Ellen shoved both hands down the back of his pants and squeezed his buttocks underneath and pushed the blue jeans down and Parker watched them wrestle naked, white skin against brown suede, eight arms and legs entwined, both crying out like they were hurt. Parker gripped the stair railings and gaped, then ran back upstairs and slid between her clean sheets. She had not told anyone.

She straightened her shoulders, out of habit, and stared out the window at the yellow strips of plastic wrapped around the trees in the Ramsay's back yard. She noticed that the little black spider had reappeared in the corner of the window and had spun one short string for a new web.

"...since you were so interested," Miss Annabelle was saying.

"Ma'am?" Parker hadn't heard what Miss Annabelle said.

"I said, I'm finished. I don't usually show my portraits to the children before their mothers see them, but I thought I'd let you take a peek. I enjoyed our little talk about painting the truth the other day."

Parker slid down from the stool. She crossed Miss Annabelle's light-filled studio slowly. To play for time, she stopped and felt the soft tips of some of Miss Annabelle's brushes standing upright in a coffee can. The bluish smoke from Miss Annabelle's cigarette hung like an island in the air.

Parker stepped past the edge of the canvas and looked at the portrait. Miss Annabelle had painted her sitting outside on a white wicker chair. Underneath a bush in the background, where you could hardly see it, was a skateboard. Her ankles were crossed and there was a smudge of dirt, barely noticeable, on one of her lace socks. The instant Parker saw her own face she realized both that her mother would be very pleased, and that this artless blonde girl with thin tanned arms was not the same person Parker had become, in only a few days, at all.

WHY I HATE PHONE SOLICITATION

Last night someone called me at dinnertime to try to sell me a cemetery plot. Well, not just one, but two; one for me and one for my wife. My wife was at the hairdresser's and I was feeding our six-month-old, who was sitting in her high chair, smearing Spaghetti-O's on her face and hair, her round blue eyes following me like searchlights.

"What with the increasing value of property, think what peace of mind you'll have once the plots are paid for," the salesman said.

"Peace of mind?" I smothered a laugh. Now, I don't exactly have a lot of peace of mind these days. In fact, like any self-employed family man, the time I don't spend working, I spend worrying. But whether I have a cemetery plot isn't what's keeping me up nights.

It's the baby. She hasn't slept more than three hours at a time since we brought her home. I've slid into a dim-witted emotionless state in which I have only one burning desire: sleep.

"Listen," I said. "People have called to try to sell me double hung insulated windows, carpet cleaning, lawn service, light bulbs, stocks, vacuum cleaner bags, and tickets to the policeman's ball. I get emails from deposed Ethiopian princes asking me for help. But this truly takes the cake. Cemetery plots. I'm getting ready to sit down to a nice dinner."

Calling Spaghetti-O's a nice dinner is like calling Steven Seagal a sensitive guy, but hell, the salesman couldn't see what I was having for dinner. I don't know, I should've hung up, but I felt like arguing with somebody. "Are you using a mailing list of potential prospects or are you just dialing random numbers? Because I'm only thirty-two years old. I mean, sure, I'm getting a few gray hairs on my chest and maybe my knees bother me a little after a set of tennis, but you've definitely got the wrong guy here."

"Of course, you're a young man, sir, but God forbid, if anything should happen, it's never too soon to think about these things. Your children will thank you for sparing them this expense." The salesman's voice was like a whirlpool, deep and liquid. I stared into my infant's round blue eyes. She smiled at me and flipped a spoonful of Spaghetti-O's neatly onto the floor. "I'm still paying OB/GYN and hospital bills." I kneeled to wipe up the O's and threw the sticky spoon in the dishwasher. "I'm reducing my standard of living on a monthly basis already so I can send this kid to college. I haven't had a full night's sleep in months. You're telling me she won't be willing to spring for a measly cemetery plot when my time comes, if need be?"

I was yelling. But it felt good to yell, and it was cheaper than therapy. I handed the baby a clean spoon, which she promptly pitched.

"What I meant to say," the salesman said, apparently without even having to breathe, "is that you can spare your children this decision at a vulnerable time. Believe it or not, there are unscrupulous people out there who will take advantage of people when they are in weakened emotional states."

"Unscrupulous people! Imagine that!" I started laughing and the baby, who likes to laugh when other people do, joined in. My wife came in from the hairdresser, her hair several inches shorter than I like it—because the baby pulls it, she says. She raised an eyebrow at our laughter.

"Who are you talking to?" she mouthed, then, when I mouthed "salesman," she knitted her brows, kissed the baby and went directly upstairs.

"Listen, buddy," I growled into the phone, "I'm warning you, unscrupulous people who hawk cemetery plots over the phone at dinnertime are going to need one themselves a lot sooner than they thought." I was proud of that one, and pinched one of the baby's toes. She was convulsed with delirious laughter and grabbed my hair in her gooey orange hands. I pried her fingers loose one by one while wedging the receiver between one hunched shoulder and my ear.

"I would never presume to take up your time, sir." The voice crooned like a siren, drawing me in. "But I happen to have only two adjacent plots available this evening. This is the only way to assure that you and your wife have plots next to each other."

Once I forgot to make seating reservations on a plane and my wife and I weren't able to sit together. We decided we could handle it for a few hours. But forever?

Then again, do we really want to be together for eternity? Our vows said "Til death do us part." Would adjoining cemetery plots, then, be an extension of our contract? Do we really want it extended? Isn't a lifetime together plenty?

Besides, while I'm perfectly happy to live in the same house and eat off the same table for decades, my wife is fond of change. Once I came home from work and my bed was facing a different direction and many of my favorite clothes were gone. I can't fathom how she'd last in the same cemetery plot, under the same rooted tree and with an unchanging view, until the end of time.

I'd been too sleep-deprived to think about how my marriage was going for quite some time. What if, years down the road, we had a bitter divorce, only to be stuck in death side by side forever, simply because we'd sprung for some sepulchral blue light special? What if we both remarried? Maybe we should check to see if two more plots adjacent to those two were available as well. And let's not forget the children. And what if our second spouses had children from their first marriage? Maybe cemetery plots were cheaper by the dozen.

My wife came back downstairs in the white terrycloth bathrobe she gave me for Christmas.

"Listen," I said to the salesman, "you're wasting your time, we're both going to be cremated."

My wife now turned to stare at me in disbelief.

"Who in the world are you talking to?" She swept by me into the kitchen. "Why do you have Spaghetti-O's in your hair? And whatever gave you the idea I wanted to be cremated? Honest to God, I can't even leave for two hours." She wiped the baby's face and hands with a damp washcloth, pulled her out of the high chair, and stood holding her, pressing her lips softly to the baby's head again and again.

I looked at the two of them, the curves of their bodies fitting together like a puzzle. Why didn't I know how she feels about cremation? And why doesn't she know how I feel?

And suddenly I have this vision of the future. My wife is older, but still slim and certainly not gray. My daughter is eighteen or so and she looks a lot like her mother did at that age and she's wearing low-slung jeans and headphones. I can't see much of myself in her although some people do say she has my feet but in this vision she's wearing black leather boots so I can't tell. There are two guys in dirty white overalls moving furniture out of the living room and my wife is saying things like "Please be careful with the secretary. It belonged to my grandmother!" and "Watch those chairs! They're Chippendales!" And I can't help but picture two cartoon chipmunks sprawled on the upholstery.

I dread seeing myself in this vision, some paunchy, grizzly guy in tennis whites with taped knees, but I never appear, which is even worse. Instead one guy in overalls picks up an unassuming urn sitting on the mantle and before anyone can say "Be careful with that!" it slips from his fingers and shatters on the hearth, spewing several cups of small gray bone-like bee-bees. My wife and daughter look at each other in horror. Then my wife says, with a sigh, "Honey, go get the Dustbuster," and my daughter glares at her and says "Why do I have to do it?"

The phone slid from my shoulder into my daughter's Spaghetti-O's. I picked it up and wiped a small collection of O's, sort of like a small beehive, off the mouthpiece.

"Honey, just tell them you're not interested." My wife was next to me now. She gently plucked a Spaghetti-O from my hair, then placed her cool raspberry lips on mine. Her shampoo had a hypnotic smell, like gardenias. The baby patted my cheek with her sticky hand.

And suddenly I remembered a summer night in the not too distant past when the baby was actually asleep and the two of us were in bed together and a breeze traveled lightly like a chiffon veil over our naked skin and we held each other in the dark. We talked about how we both hate disco, how our fathers both tear up when watching *Bridge Over the River Kwai*, and how our daughter looks like an angel, particularly, most especially, when she is asleep.

"Like I said, you're wasting your time," I told the salesman.

"No problem," he said. "I'll try back later." As I hung up, I thought I heard a nasty chuckle. I expect he will get back to me, sooner or later. Those guys just never give up.

THE HOMEPLACE

Miles had been saving for the August weekend getaway for a year, since just after Betsy's miscarriage. Betsy had said her parents used to go to this resort, and leave her and her sister at home. Thus the place had a forbidden mythology that had always intrigued her, but Miles and Betsy had never even considered going because of the cost. Miles was absolutely sure his own parents had never heard of the place. Then a serendipitous thing had happened: a business meeting at the resort had been scheduled for the same weekend as their fifth anniversary. His company agreed to pay for the nights of the meeting, and he made reservations for two extra nights. He called a sitter, home from college, to babysit for their son, Cameron. When his plans were complete he had a feeling of great satisfaction.

Yet, on the way to the resort Betsy cried twice in the car.

She'd been crying at odd times over the miscarriage for the past year. Miles was not as worried as Betsy about their ability to conceive another child; two-year-old Cameron was such a handful Miles' worries were more along the lines of being able to handle another one. Betsy had seemed to get over it after a few teary months, and had gone back to teaching, but then this past June school let out, the due date for the baby had passed, and Betsy had drifted back into despair.

Miles pulled over into an antique gas station beside the mountain road and put his hand on his wife's shoulder. "I know," he said. "I think about it, too."

Betsy looked at her lap. Her thick dark lashes framed her blue-green eyes like a thicket. Miles was always looking into them to see if he could possibly understand what she was thinking, usually without success. After knowing Betsy for eight years now, he had come to the conclusion that his mind worked nothing like hers, yet he still tried to guess. Now, when she glanced up at him skeptically, he guessed that she didn't believe that he thought about the baby and he wished somehow he could prove that he did. Of course he'd been grieved. What grieved Betsy grieved Miles.

After a time, she stopped crying and they moved on.

Closer to the resort, high in the mountains, as they traversed the narrow switchbacks, the hood of the car rose before them and the side of the mountain fell away on Miles' side in a cascade of rocks and the sun-dappled, hand-like leaves of thousands of oaks. Beside Betsy rose a sheer towering wall the color of dried blood, etched by eons of thin streams.

"Slow down, Miles!" Betsy said in a near-whisper. "There's not even a guard rail."

"It's OK, there's a whole lane over there, and I've driven these mountains plenty of times before," Miles assured her, and concentrated on showing her how smoothly and rhythmically he cut the wheel to take the turns.

"Stop," she said. "You have to stop."

"There's nowhere to pull over, Betsy," he said, feeling a little impatient now. "And any minute there could be someone behind me."

"There's no one!" she cried, and suddenly she put her hands over her face and sobbed. Her sobs seemed louder in the closeness of the car.

Miles had planned for months for this weekend. He'd pictured her walking into the well-appointed room he'd studied on the web site; maybe he would even put his hands over her eyes and reveal the magnificent view of the valley from the soaring Palladian windows. He had pictured her exclaiming over the Champagne and the marble in the bathroom and the heavy luxury of the matching white chenille bathrobes (also shown on the web site).

He hadn't planned for sobbing on the mountain road on the way. There wasn't a thing he could do. He didn't think he could spare a hand from the wheel even to pat her knee. So he continued to drive. Soon her gasps subsided into soft staccato sniffles and finally silence.

But when they drove up to the imposing red brick hotel, and into the circular turnaround, and a valet in an eggplant-colored jacket sprinted down from beside a gleaming white column on the porch to open Betsy's door, Miles regained hope.

"Good afternoon, welcome to the Homeplace," said the valet, holding a gloved hand out for Betsy. And before Miles knew it, two uniformed men had unloaded his trunk and relieved him of his car keys. He and Betsy stood on the steps, watching well-groomed folks in white rocking chairs drinking iced tea and swapping stories. Miles was not one for telling stories himself. Give him a golf club. Give him any kind of ball. Do not give him an empty afternoon and ask him to fill it with stories.

"May we store your clubs in the pro shop for you, sir?" asked the second valet, shouldering Miles' bag, which Miles now realized was dirty and worn. One of his head covers had a rip in it.

Miles wished that he had replaced at least the head cover, if not the bag before the trip but immediately squelched the wish, thinking, *There is nothing wrong with my goddamn golf bag.* "Certainly," he replied, with a great deal of dignity.

Fortunately, Betsy was standing a few feet away with the luggage, chatting with the valet, when Miles checked in and learned that apparently his company had not paid for the first two nights, as his boss Jim said he would. Miles rubbed his index finger over a blood vessel in his temple that suddenly ached. Jim was always so agreeable and jovial and then later you'd find that he hadn't done what he said he'd do. It was possible Miles could call him from the room. Maybe Jim just forgot. It was also possible, however, that Jim had decided he simply wasn't paying for it, in which case calling later from the room wouldn't do any good. Jim wouldn't exactly refuse to pay; he'd just neglect to take the call and then continue to forget until Miles gave up.

"Maybe they were planning to reimburse you," the desk clerk said with a tight smile. She had long ago licked all the lipstick from her lips; the hotel was sold out this weekend. "Do you have a credit card we can put on record, sir?"

Miles reached into his wallet and pulled out his debit card. He had saved every penny that would be required for the two extra nights he'd reserved. Yet the amount on his card wasn't sufficient to cover the two nights Jim had promised to pay. He felt slight dampness at his hairline and under his armpits.

"Is this a debit card, sir?"

At that moment he noticed a sign on the counter saying that the hotel did not accept debit cards, only credit cards. He did have a credit card, but the limit did not approach the amount that would be required to cover four nights in this resort. Miles glanced at Betsy and gave her a casual smile.

She smiled back. Her tears were gone and she was enjoying her conversation with the valet. Betsy was good at getting to know people. By the time they got to the room, assuming they got there, Betsy would know where the valet had gone to high school, what the mascot was, the valet's wife's birthday, and scads of other minutiae about him. The valet would be their friend for the entire weekend and would offer eager hello's, trying to catch Betsy's eye all the while. Miles knew; he had seen this happen many times.

"I have a credit card right here," Miles said with his best poker face, handing it across the dark marble counter. Maybe the clerk wouldn't check the limit until they checked out, and by then Miles could figure something out. He tried to calm himself by simply counting the number of times his heart beat before she handed back the card.

"Thank you, sir."

Relief flooded his limbs like water. He shoved his wallet in his pocket. "All set!" he called to Betsy in an off-hand way.

Their room was in the Garden Wing, and it was a long walk. The valet's name was R.P. and his wife was a bookkeeper. Both of their sons were wrestlers. R.P. was a Nascar fan and especially liked Jeff Gordon. Miles tuned out of the conversation and admired various aspects of the garden hall, such as the thick green and white carpeting, the lovely way the light played over a set of crystal chess pieces, and a long flawless row of copper-colored day lilies outside the floor to ceiling windows.

As he entered the room, Miles held his breath. Sometimes Betsy didn't like the view and wanted to change. Today, with the crying, he was prepared for the worst. The bed was large—a king—and the comforter appeared clean. Miles glanced out the window. The view was of part of the roof of a floor below. Uh-oh.

"Miles," said Betsy, and Miles steeled himself. But, "Should we try hiking?" was what Betsy said. "R.P. says you can see the whole valley from Deer Lick hiking trail."

Miles hated hiking. If you were going to walk a long distance, at least swing a golf club or shoot something. Miles had already planned that he would play golf while Betsy sat by the pool.

"We'll see," he said, reaching for his wallet. Then he realized Betsy was already tipping the bellman much more than he ever would. Since Miles' conference had already begun, he had no choice except to give Betsy a hurried kiss, and head downstairs to the meeting room.

After R.P. showed Betsy how to work the air conditioning, pointed out the benefits of the servibar, regaled her with highlights of his son's last wrestling match, and she was finally alone, Betsy wandered around the room, running her fingers over the soft cotton comforter, the smooth bar of gelatin soap in the bathroom, and the fluffy white towels in the powder room. She wrapped the chenille bathrobe tightly around herself, over her clothes, and went to the window, looked down over the roof below, and watched a few people rocking languidly on the front porch. Normally, in her head, she would be able to hear the tinkle of the ice in their tea, and hear the rhythmic scrape and squeak of the rocking chairs, but today she watched as though inside a glass bubble. She lay on the bed and stared at the ceiling.

What was wrong with her?

Look at this lovely place. Look at all the trouble that Miles had gone to. Look at all the money this was costing. She didn't deserve Miles doing all this. She had been such a terrible wife and mother this past year, ever since the miscarriage. She could hardly make herself clean the house or go to the store. She knew she was no fun to be with.

She closed her eyes. She thought of Cameron, and the thought only made her feel tired. She thought of two of her students at school, little girls who were smart and spunky and asked questions all the time, girls that she thought her lost daughter might have grown up to be like. And soon they'd stop asking questions. Stop being themselves and start doing things for the benefit of the boys. It just all made her feel sad and tired.

She'd been reading this book about depression, though, and the author had written that you had to make yourself do things. He claimed that changing your thoughts could change your moods and thus you could lift yourself by sheer will out of despair. She'd been doing some of his exercises, and the hike seemed just the thing. You were supposed to write down negative thoughts such as "I am dreading going on that hike," and then write down the counteraction of the thought. "But after I get started and I get moving I'll probably feel a lot better. The views will be gorgeous. The fresh air will be great." And so on. The more tired and unenthusiastic she felt about the hike, the more determined she was to go.

She already knew, however, that Miles would not want to go on the hike. She went into the powder room and sipped a glass of cool water as she looked at herself in the mirror. She had never lost the five pounds from the pregnancy. Her eyes had dark rings around them. She looked older than thirty-two.

All she wanted to do was lie on the bed in this bathrobe, but she forced herself to put on her bathing suit. The indoor pool was fed by mineral springs, the brochure said, and people had been coming here for the healing benefit of those springs since the1700's. She slipped her bathing suit cover up over her head, gathered her book and purse, and headed down the long hallway. Maybe the springs would heal her.

The indoor pool sparkled with prisms of greenish light reflecting from rows of green tiles lining the sides and pool deck, and from the beveled glass ceiling arching over like a covered glass dish. Normally with indoor pools the chlorine smell was strong but here it was faint, barely present. Outside the pool structure was a patio for sunning. The water was warm—maintained at ninety degrees by the springs—and Betsy felt her body become weightless and one with the water as she let herself float aimlessly. She hadn't felt in harmony with anything for a long time and on her skin, the water felt like the sheerest silk. Outside on the patio she wrapped herself in a thick towel, shut her eyes, let the sun's orange glow penetrate the inside of her eyelids, and she drifted off.

Yet within a few minutes the fussing of a baby wriggled through her formless dreams, and a mother's soliloquy wove itself into Betsy's ear. "I have to take care of Joey right now, Caroline, and you'll have to put on your swimmies all by yourself. Joey needs me to feed him and hold him and that takes both of my hands. You're a big girl, you can put on your swimmies and you can go over and walk down the steps into the pool."

Betsy opened one eye to look at the young mother. Her hair was flat and greasy and her face was expressionless with exhaustion. The mother kept talking to the little girl, coaxing her, and the little girl stood by her with her stomach sticking out, one hand gripping her mother's knee. The baby's wails did not abate. His face was red and smeared with fury.

Betsy sat up and smiled at the little girl. "How about if I help you with your swimmies? Will that be OK, while your mommy feeds the baby?"

With one finger in her mouth, the little girl appraised Betsy, looking her up and down. At first she shook her head and edged closer to her mother, but at last she gave a tiny nod of her head and held one of the swimmies out to Betsy.

Betsy was in the water a few minutes later with the little girl as she splashed and dove. She took a few pennies from her wallet and threw them for the girl to retrieve. Cameron loved this game. At some point Betsy began to cry, but she ducked her face frequently underwater so it wouldn't be noticed, as she tossed pennies to the girl. When she played with Cameron, he was indefatigable, jumping into the water again and again until he was waterlogged, but the little girl lost interest more quickly. Behind them, Betsy heard the baby's cries change to whimpers and then sighs of relief and gratitude. The mother fell asleep while feeding the baby, her head lolling onto her shoulder, and Betsy propped a towel there and sat on the edge of the pool and she and the little girl began playing tic-tac-toe, drawing fleeting x's and o's onto the light green tiles with their wet fingers.

Miles got a break from his conference and hurried back to the room to check on Betsy, but the room was empty and she'd not left him a note. He tried calling her cell phone but she didn't answer. Someone at the conference had mentioned that the pro shop charged ten dollars a day to store your clubs and that valet parking was fifteen dollars a day. Miles had decided he had to get his sticks back and move the car, even if he had to miss most of a lecture.

Racing the half mile back from the self-parking lot, Miles worked up a sweat, and then he hiked to the pro shop, which was at least another half mile, to retrieve his clubs, and carried them back to the room. The grounds of this resort were endless. He was adding distance because he was avoiding the check-in desk out of fear that the clerk might try to run his card and see the limit and try to wave him down. Once, walking down one of the long halls, he went the wrong way. He was completely worn out and it wasn't even dinnertime.

Hurrying down the corridor afterward, drenched in sweat, searching for Betsy, he saw the bellman, who volunteered that he'd seen her heading down the hall in a bathing suit cover-up. Miles immediately wondered if the bellman had a more than ordinary interest in his wife, since he had noticed her in the hall and also noticed what she had been wearing.

"I'll go by myself, then," said Betsy, trying to keep her voice steady and reasonable.

"You're not going on a hike up the side of a mountain by yourself." They had had a terrible and agonizingly expensive dinner in the hotel dining room, where the air conditioning had been pumped up to such a level that Betsy's fingers and toes had gone numb, they had each had some wine, and now the argument that had been bearing down on them like a thunderhead filling the sky finally arrived.

"Why not? I'm not some fainting flower. You don't want to go, and I do, so I'll just go."

"It's not that I don't want to go, it's just that I already pre-paid to play in this conference tournament. The money is already spent." Miles had then used a very patronizing tone of voice with her. "The golf courses here are world-famous, Betsy. It would be absurd, as a golfer, for me to come to the Homeplace, and not play golf."

"Then go ahead and play. I'm not saying a word about you playing. And I'll go on the hike."

Miles stood up, balled up his golf shirt, and threw it on the floor. "Goddammit, Betsy, I can't let you hike up the mountain by yourself. Why can't you go to the pool and maybe we can do the hike the next day—although I have lectures all day and I don't know which one I can miss."

"I went to the pool today. I don't want to go to the pool tomorrow. I want to go on the hike." Betsy usually backed down by now but she had determined that she had to go on this hike. She didn't want to go any more than Miles did be but she had to, for the sake of her sanity, it seemed. "I'm perfectly capable of hiking by myself."

She started to pick up and fold Miles' shirt, but glared at him and left it there. She went in the bathroom and shut the door.

Miles was paired with a married couple. The woman had breast enhancements, which were attractive in a symmetrical way but certainly did little for her golf swing. The man had a baseball swing that would never produce anything but a hook, which is exactly what he hit on the first tee. Miles heaved a sigh, removed his head covers and put two Titleists and a handful of tees into his pocket before stepping up to the tee box. He had a deflated feeling, as though this game of golf that he had fought so hard for had lost its luster.

I refuse to feel guilty about one lousy game of golf at a world-famous course, he thought. There were so many jokes about men playing golf to escape their wives. Like the joke about the man sneaking into the house one morning and climbing in bed to join his wife and the wife saying, "You can't fool me. I know what you've been doing."

And the man saying, "You're right, I admit it, Lorraine, I have a lover. I'm sorry, I made a terrible mistake, please forgive me, I'll break it off immediately."

And the wife saying, "You big liar. You were playing golf."

This was truly a first in the five years they had been married: they would be pursuing separate activities on the very day of their anniversary. Was this a portent of things to come?

Miles' drive hooked left, veering dangerously close to the hiking trail that meandered down the left side of the fairway. He refused to become discouraged. He focused on the lush but immaculately trimmed grass as he drove up the hill toward the green.

The sign at the trail head took Betsy aback, and she kneeled to adjust her sock in her running shoe as she decided what to do. It said, "Please be wary of bears in the vicinity." The description of what you should do if you encountered a bear on the trail was uncomfortably long. The sign warned you to make plenty of noise to announce your presence. If you did happen to see a bear, the sign warned, make no sudden movements and do not make eye contact with the bear. Stay still for a few moments, then back away slowly, without turning your back on the bear. If the bear should rush you, the sign said, you should fight back, making the loudest noise possible.

Betsy retied her shoe. Maybe she should just go to the pool as Miles wanted her to do. A metallic taste came into her mouth and she stood up. She twisted the top on her bottle of water open, then closed, several times, thinking.

Really, what were the chances she would see a bear? The resort probably was required by law to put up signs such as these. Probably no bears had been seen in the vicinity in years. The resort was just covering its ass.

She twisted the cap from the water bottle, took a swig, and headed up the trail.

The trail seemed, ironically, to be meandering along beside the golf course. This morning Miles had pecked her cheek and mumbled "Happy Anniversary" on his way to his meeting and she'd pretended not to wake up. She'd dawdled while getting ready to go on the hike, thinking he might come back to the room, saying he'd changed his mind, but he hadn't. So the day of their anniversary was slipping by and they hadn't even spoken. That kiss had been completely perfunctory.

Beside the trail she saw a sweet sunny clump of daisies, and, with determination, she picked one and fastened it behind her ear. Just because she was alone didn't mean she couldn't enjoy herself. As she climbed upward, the muscles in her calves tightened and she found herself leaning forward and breathing a little more heavily, but she kept up her pace and took pleasure in recognizing the goldenrod and Queen Anne's lace beside the path.

The depression book was right. Getting out and moving around was helping. Much of her problem was certainly hormonal, as well. For nearly twelve weeks, her body had been filling with pregnancy hormones, and it was taking months for it to get back to normal. In Miles defense, he had been trying hard to understand and to help her. He didn't know what to do. And no wonder, since she herself had no idea what, other than a baby, might make things right.

And sometimes she'd think about a baby and even then she'd still feel tired and hopeless. The young mother at the pool had been so drained. Her voice had sounded as though it was on autopilot, worn into a monotone groove of talking to the little girl while trying to care for the baby. There didn't seem to be joy there, just exhaustion. Betsy wondered if the young mother was also working. She wondered where, at this fabulous resort, the father was. Maybe playing golf, leaving his exhausted wife to struggle with the children.

Betsy deliberately kept up her pace. The pine needles felt springy beneath her feet and the path climbed relentlessly upward and patches of sun shot through the trees. A trickle of sweat ran between her breasts.

But why shouldn't a young father be able to play golf? He was tired and needed a break, too. These seemed like such old questions, like questions that people struggled with in the 1950s. Why hadn't they been solved by now?

As she meandered along, she realized she hadn't given up hope that Miles would quit the golf game and come racing up the hiking trail after her. But she realized that even if he did, she would not act glad to see him, even if she was.

Miles was playing like shit. And of course all you have to do is allow yourself to think about playing like shit and then you're doomed to play like shit for the rest of the round. Golf was such a damn mind game.

He hit a particularly bad shot in which the ball popped into the air and attained enormous height while achieving distance of only fifty yards and then looked over and saw, on the hiking trail beside the golf course, a beautiful dark-haired woman walking along the trail. The way she moved reminded him immensely of Betsy. And then he realized that it *was* Betsy.

Watching her walk, his mind momentarily left his golf game. He knew her well enough to know that she was preoccupied, thinking about something, but making an effort to enjoy her surroundings as she walked. It certainly never used to be an effort. He could remember nights at dinner or at plays or movies when they were first dating where she laughed all night and he couldn't take his eyes off her.

There! She seemed as though she had looked over. He waved. But she didn't wave back.

Was she still mad? Maybe she hadn't seen him.

The hike was much longer than she had anticipated, and much steeper. She lost her breath and pain shot through her calves. There were times when she was literally grasping at the limbs of trees to pull herself up to the next level, stumbling and slipping over layered tree roots.

At last she emerged at the top of the mountain, where hikers could sit on an outcropping of rocks and admire the view of the resort and the valley below. Cooler air wafted across the curve of her neck. Betsy froze as goose bumps ran up the back of her arms.

She'd had no idea she was so high. She wanted to walk out and look over the edge but the same vertigo that had overtaken her when Miles had been driving the switchbacks overtook her now. Finally she dropped to her knees and inched her way closer to the edge.

Lightheaded, she gasped a shallow breath of the cool air and sat back on her heels, feeling a heady combination of euphoria and terror. The resort looked lovely from here. You couldn't hear the babies crying, or see the long lines of tired people waiting to speak to the concierge or the people freezing to death in the dining room. You saw only the emerald expanse of grass and the rising white-columned brick structure, and the tiny people leaping nimbly about on the tennis courts.

Here she was at this beautiful resort and all she could do was think, with a shameful sense of guilt that lay across her chest like a lead apron, about how she didn't deserve any of it.

Behind her Betsy heard a sound and thought 'Miles!" and turned around just as the sound sorted itself into something like the cry of a frustrated baby. It was not unlike one of the cries uttered by little Joey the day before when she was playing tic-tac-toe with his sister.

On the edge of the path where she was headed was a small rather forlorn-looking animal that she thought at first was a medium-sized dog. Its ears poked out, too large for its head, and its feet were too big, with black fur draping large claws. Its fur was a fuzzy black, and it had a tan snout with a black stripe along its top. It looked at Betsy with curiosity, through small, opaque eyes, raising its snout and sniffing the air, and then began to amble with a rolling, pigeon-toed gait in her direction.

Betsy was already close to the edge of the rocks—closer than she ever meant to go—and could not go any further.

Mama might be somewhere close. Oh God what had the sign said. Remain still, and do not make eye contact. But the cub was just ambling toward her in an unconcerned way, as if they were fast friends from a previous life. Betsy remained perfectly still but her heart beat so hard she thought it might leap right out of her throat and lie on one of the rusty-looking rocks, contracting.

And now the cub was a few feet away and it stood on its hind legs, still sniffing, took two steps toward her, and because she had no room to back away, leaned heavily against her. It had a rank, sharp wild animal smell. Hardly breathing, Betsy looked at the claws at her waist. She and the cub seemed to be dancing in a bizarre way. The cub kept its snout in the air and nosed her water bottle. For one harrowing, fainting moment she held the bottle out and the cub took it in its jaws and slid down to all fours again. Betsy thought she might collapse, but then the cub began playing with the water bottle, rolling around on the rocks, batting it with its feet, and gnawing at it.

Shaking ferociously, Betsy took one step back toward the path. She glanced up into the woods to see if the mother was anywhere near, and saw nothing. She took another very slow and deliberate step back, and within a moment or two she was back on the path. Her mouth was so dry her tongue was stuck to the bottom of her mouth, and she thought that any moment she might simply fall to her knees from fear. Yet still she put one foot in front of another and soon the trail was heading down the other side of the mountain.

What if the mother bear had been there? How could she and Miles have gone their entire anniversary without speaking to each other? What if Betsy had been mauled or killed, and she had never had a chance to make up with Miles? All she could think about was wanting to tell Miles about this. And what if she didn't have him to tell?

Breathing heavily, she remained in control enough not to run for nearly twenty minutes before the severe shaking of her limbs began to quiet down and she was able to catch her breath.

Once safely back on the grounds of the resort, she felt so weak she sat down on a bench. Coming up the brick path was the little girl from the pool with her mother, who was pushing a stroller. Betsy, taking a deep, trembling breath, summoned a smile. Both mother and daughter walked by, staring at Betsy as though they'd never seen her before.

After his abysmal golf round Miles returned to the room and drank a beer out of the servibar though he had once told Betsy that hell would freeze over before he would do such a thing. He saw a message on the hotel phone, but didn't pick it up because if could be only one thing: the front desk calling about his card. Was the card already maxed out? Miles downed his beer, considering his options.

He called Jim, to remind him of his offer to pay, but Jim, characteristically, did not pick up his phone.

His mind kept returning to the moment when he had waved at Betsy, and thought she saw him, but she hadn't waved back. He'd known she was mad but assumed she'd get over it. Maybe she hadn't gotten over it. Maybe she was in a hormonal state where logic was not part of the equation. He felt anger swelling again, and a slight feeling of fear. Was he now going to have to spend every waking minute of the rest of his life worrying about his wife's state of mind?

Yet, the way she had simply walked on when he'd seen her on the golf course haunted him. What if something in her had just snapped; what if the experiences of the past year and the things he'd said during the fight had simply erased the feelings she'd had for him? She hadn't acted really loving toward him in a long time. A year ago he would have thought that impossible but now he was not sure at all. He felt a stab of panic at the thought.

The door opened and Betsy came in, with high color in her cheeks, her breasts heaving. She had a flower in her hair. Things like that always got him.

"Miles! You're here! Miles, I saw a baby bear. It came right up to me and took my water bottle. It gave me a bear hug. "

Betsy looked different from the Betsy he'd grown used to over the past year—her features were alive and passionate and awake.

"A bear!" He crossed the room and put a hand on each arm. "You're OK? It didn't hurt you?"

"It hugged me." Her eyes sparked and her mouth was open with excitement. "I'm fine. Miles, I'm so sorry. All I could think was, what if I died and we had never made up?" She stood there with the flower in her hair. "It's our anniversary. I just want to…"

Miles wrapped his arms tightly around her. He could feel her heart beating next to his body. "Sorry, I'm kind of sweaty," he said after a moment.

"So am I." Her voice was muffled in his shirt. "I like the smell of your sweat. Don't you like mine?"

"I always like the way you smell." Miles realized he was about to cry.

But then the phone rang.

"Don't answer it," he said. He passed the alcove with the bathroom and threw the dead bolt on the door.

"Why not?"

"Just don't."

"OK," Betsy said, and Miles stepped closer to her and put his arms around her again and said, "Is this how the bear hugged you?" and she said "Yes, sort of, except he was very small, you know, his claws reached just to my waist." And so he put his hands around her waist—he had always loved the way he could almost put them around - except when she'd been pregnant with Cameron- and he said, "Like that?" And she said, "Yes, like that."

Then Miles was removing her T-shirt and then her bra and when her hands moved up his chest inside his sweat-stained golf shirt he took it as a sure sign and he cupped her breasts in both hands.

"Wait, my hiking shoes," she said as they tumbled onto the bed, and she sat up to untie them while he stroked her back. He briefly thought to make it lovely and slow, since it was their anniversary, but could not. He had buried himself deep inside her with his nose in the valley of her neck when there was an insistent knock on the door.

"Miles…" said Betsy.

"Ignore it," he said, moving over her, breathing into her hair.

"OK," she said, and she wrapped her legs around him but then the knock came again.

"Don't open it," he gasped.

The knock again.

Betsy stopped moving but Miles did not. He kept his eyes closed and concentrated, pushing everything from his brain except the smell of Betsy's neck. Just a bit farther to go, just a little bit. And then Betsy arched her back and that was it. He thought he might plow straight through the earth to the other side. They both lay there breathing hard, letting the moment spin out and out. After the sorrow of the last year, Miles felt such relief and wonder that his eyes and throat began to burn. He felt something wet on his cheek and realized Betsy was crying too. Wordless, he lay there and held her. He thought again about seeing Betsy today on the hiking trail and not realizing at first who she was. He marveled that he could not know his own wife, but reflected that marriage could be like that; sometimes your spouse seemed to be a different person entirely.

"Happy anniversary," he whispered as he settled next to her. "Hey, today, when you were hiking, did you see me wave at you? I saw you walking beside the golf course and I waved."

Betsy opened her eyes. "You saw me while I was hiking?"

"Yes. I didn't know it was you at first. I thought it was a beautiful dark-haired woman."

"You were lusting after another woman only it was me."

"It was you, yes." He gave her a soft kiss.

She took his face in her hands and kissed him back, then pulled his head to her chest and stroked his head. "Poor Miles," she said.

"What do you mean, poor Miles?"

"This last year," she said. They were silent, breathing in each other's arms, for several minutes. He felt his heart lightening with hope for the first time in many months. At last she said, "Give me that pillow, put it under me," and she pulled her knees to her chest and he helped her wedge the pillow under her hips. "I'm just going to lie here for about ten minutes," she said. "Can't hurt."

Miles sat up. "I have an idea," he said. It had occurred to him that if they checked out now, the card would cover what they had done so far. "Why don't we just pack up and go home? This place isn't for us."

Betsy looked at him, her cheek against the pillow. "Why?" she said. "I was just starting to have fun."

And then Miles thought, *I should just tell her about the money. She's my wife.*

Then Betsy shrugged and said, "I know Cameron misses us. Only I can't get up for at least ten minutes."

"I'll pack, you lie there," Miles said, amazed that he had suggested leaving and that Betsy had agreed so easily.

Betsy started singing "Let's Give 'Em Something to Talk About," while lying in the fetal position with her hips propped in the air while Miles, mostly naked, stuffed his golf shoes down into his golf bag, tossed his dirty golf clothes into his suitcase, and zipped Betsy's overnight case. Betsy sang to Cameron all the time now, but had been a long time since Betsy had sung to Miles. By the time Betsy finished the song he was packed and dressed and Betsy finally stretched out her legs and said, "OK!" and got up and went to the bathroom.

"Listen," he said. "I'm going to take most of the luggage and head down to the front desk to check out. Want to meet me in the self-parking lot?"

Out in the hall, two doors down, he saw a cart laden with towels and soaps. Perhaps the knock on the door had been housekeeping, not the front desk. And maybe the call in the room had been Jim, or the babysitter. He felt foolish, but the decision was made now.

By the desk, Miles stood before the same clerk who had checked him in the day before. Her lipstick was still in evidence today and she seemed in a better humor. He felt considerably more in control. He was seventy percent sure the card would cover it.

"Any particular reason you're checking out early, sir?"

"Homesick," he said, smiling.

"Here you are, sir," she said, handing him the receipt.

He felt so relieved he grabbed the receipt with a comical flourish to disguise his hand's tremor. He stuffed it in his pocket, and left the porch and the people in the rocking chairs. The weight of the two suitcases was evenly distributed in his hands, and not one of the bellmen offered a bit of help. Not that he wanted it.

He saw Betsy from afar crossing the parking lot with the duffle bag and his heart contracted. She still had no bounce in her step like the old Betsy. Watching her walk now, the concentrated effort she was making, putting one foot in front of the other with such intense determination, filled him with love for her.

He should tell her about the card, about why they really checked out. They'd been married five years now. But considering her tears on the way up the mountain, the car on the way home wasn't the place. And once they got home, they would have their hands full with Cameron. Well, later. He'd tell her later.

MUST REMAIN ANONYMOUS

Darla was the first to arrive, and took her usual plastic chair in the cold, mildewed basement of Moorestown Methodist Church. When she pulled out her cell phone to switch it to vibrate, she saw that she'd gotten another message. She wasn't supposed to open it. But she couldn't resist. It said:

> Most Esteemed dltucker10023:
> I am a representative in a highly confidential matter in which a deposed Royal Family which must remain anonymous must leave bank accounts in excess of thirty million dollars. These monies require a U.S. fiscal agent and all that is required is your name and bank account number.

Darla imagined a family in Biblical-looking blue satin or—no, wait, white cotton robes—being smuggled through a crumbling underground tunnel. A mother and father, a daughter, and a boy, all weeping, being led by a dark-skinned person in camouflage fatigues and brandishing a torch. These things happened all the time, they really did.

Darla took a deep breath. Last time, she'd given her savings number and her account had been emptied. The time before that, a jet ski and a wide screen TV had been charged on her credit card. At first she'd been upset, but then thought, *But they need it so much more than I do.* The group members had been trying to persuade her that if she resisted, she'd be able to afford her rent and car payments. She couldn't ask Dad for help again and even Aunt Elsie had started screening her calls.

Darla deleted the message, assuring herself that the family would be saved, someone else would help them. She took pride in the fact that she did so with less hesitation and yearning than just last week. As she slid her cell phone into her purse, a shadow darkened the floor outside the doorway. She hoped it was William, so they'd get a moment or two alone, but it was Johnny.

"Hi," she said. Johnny nodded in a definitely hostile way as he crossed the room, then slumped in a chair halfway around the circle from her, thrusting his pelvis to the edge of the seat. He crossed his arms over his chest, and looked at his watch. Darla knew he thought she was ridiculously naïve for falling for all those spam emails. Well, she thought he was disgusting.

Johnny's last escapade had been trying to eat the most hog eyeballs in two minutes on a survival show. On the tape he'd shown the group his first meeting, people crowded around him cheering him on, screaming his name, "JohnNY! JohnNY!" Seconds later they groaned and turned away in disgust when he vomited into the yellow bucket next to the table, and the camera caught it all on tape. After that, he'd lost the contest, and then, wildly swinging the yellow bucket, attacked the host of the show. The judge in the assault case made him come to this group. Johnny had smooth Italian skin, honed muscles, and passionate liquid brown eyes. Darla found it hard to reconcile her revulsion to his personality with his physical attractiveness.

Footsteps sounded on the stairs, and Darla glanced at the doorway, hoping again to see William's yearning eyes, but Chad, the group leader, came in. Darla smiled.

"Darla, nice to see you." Chad's movements had a spasmodic jerkiness, as if he were receiving tiny electric shocks.

"You, too." Darla folded her hands in her lap.

"How ya doin." Johnny looked at Chad but didn't smile.

"Good, Johnny, you?" Chad's voice held falsely effusive enthusiasm. He pushed his glasses up on his nose, opened his notebook, and clicked his mechanical pencil. "We'll wait a few minutes before we start." He flipped through his notes from last week. "Does anyone know if William is coming tonight?"

Johnny shrugged.

Darla shook her head, tightening her lips. Before they found the church, they'd met once at William's house. He lived in a clapboard rooming house with a sagging front porch in an old part of town. William had given them each one of his flimsy self-published poetry books as they left the meeting. The past week she'd read one of his poems each day. The one yesterday was about a beach vacation with family members who weren't speaking to each other.

"Ah! There he is!" Chad said.

The heat of a blush spread up Darla's neck like an Elizabethan collar. William was thin, unhealthy and disheveled-looking, with longish dark hair that needed washing, and his entire being was imbued with the stale smell of pot, but Darla could tell he was good-hearted. As he crossed to his seat, a scrap of yellow lined paper fell on the floor, and he picked it up, shoving it into the pocket of his wrinkled pants. William was always writing his ideas on these scraps of paper, though he was supposed to stop; that was precisely why he was coming to the group.

"William, glad you made it. Why don't we get started?" Chad said. "I'd like to say that as group leader I want to keep strict control over the direction of today's meeting. I take personal responsibility for what happened last week, and I don't intend to let it happen again."

Last week William had teased Johnny, and Johnny, who was surprisingly sensitive about some things, had lost his temper with William. Reverend Melton had been forced to interrupt, asking the group to quiet down.

"I'll start," Chad continued, "by reporting on my own progress this week. Good news and bad news." He reached into his briefcase and pulled out a tattered roll of posters. The rubber band snapped as Chad unrolled a torn poster featuring a photo of himself, with the headline, *Don't leave Chad hanging! Chad for County Commissioner!* Someone had scrawled "I am a huge tool" with magic marker in a cartoon balloon coming from Chad's mouth. "The good news is, I've collected these from around town. I think I've retrieved every one."

"That must have been hard for you, Chad," Darla said, pretending not to see the graffiti.

"It was," Chad said, blinking fiercely. "The schools need more money. Teachers should be paid better, and developers need to help pay for roads and other infrastructure. Recycling must be increased. Graft and corruption and gerrymandering must go. This can all be done if a few truly dedicated people get in there."

"But you've been defeated four times," William said.

"Did you know that you can look at the county budget online? Did you know that every single line item is available for public scrutiny?" Chad's Adam's apple bobbed with righteous fury.

Darla knew that Chad's heart was in the right place. But he looked so geeky, and he didn't speak well. Worst of all, he didn't have business connections. In the last election Chad had received only three votes.

"Just curious—what's the bad news?" William asked.

"The bad news?" Chad repeated. "Oh, I've tried to withdraw from the county commissioner race, and they won't let me. My name is already on the ballot. Apparently even dying can't get your name off once it's there. Oh, and my house was repossessed. And my wife left me. That hurt, but what's really devastating was learning that Sally didn't even vote for me in the last election."

"You knew that, Chad," Darla said, injecting a tough realism into her voice. "Sally told you she didn't vote for you. And she told you if you ran again she would leave you."

Chad sighed. 'I guess I just didn't believe her." The posters slid to the floor. "I was hoping that if I withdrew from the race, she'd come back. But she said it's over."

"Where are you living now?" Darla asked tenderly.

"Above my stationery store downtown."

Darla and William nodded in silent sympathy. Johnny looked at the ceiling.

"Do you need pots and pans?" Darla asked.

"No, no, I'm fine," Chad said heartily. "Enough about me. William? Have you managed to stop writing?"

William glanced at Darla before he answered. "I have managed not to write at all in my waking hours. But apparently I got up last night and started another novel in my sleep. I swear I have no memory of it. But there were fifteen printed pages lying on my desk when I woke up."

"And you're sure you wrote them?" Darla couldn't help but ask.

"Well, unless my cat recently learned to type," said William. Darla's feelings were hurt by the smart aleck nature of his response.

"OK, so let's see, that's your fifteenth unpublished novel?" Chad said, referring to his notes.

"Yes," said William defensively. "And I did have an ethical question. Before I started coming to this group, I sent query letters out to more than two dozen agents, and I got a request for a full manuscript yesterday. Shouldn't I respond, since I sent the query *before* I started the group?"

"You really shouldn't," said Chad. "If you're sincere about trying to quit."

William nodded glumly. "I do have one piece of interesting news. I gave you each a copy of my self-published poetry books, and I still have three hundred left, so I left them outside the grocery store, with a sign saying 'Free.' Well, someone took one! And, so, even though I'm definitely not going to write anymore, one person is reading my work."

"That's fantastic, William!" Darla said.

"You have no idea how fulfilling that is. To think that even one person might be connecting with my work. To think it might make a difference in someone's life."

"And I'm sure it is making a difference," Darla said with as much encouragement as she dared. She wanted to talk to him about his poems, but not in front of the group.

"You know this is hopeless, don't you William?" Chad said. William had been fired from two jobs for working on his novels when he was supposed to be entering sales data.

But sometimes when William talked about an idea, Darla found herself thinking, *Wow, that's a wonderful story.* There's heroism there. Some of his stories made her cry. She sometimes wondered why he couldn't just keep writing them, even if a publisher never wanted to publish them. But this wasn't the kind of thing you were supposed to say in the group.

Johnny cleared his throat and looked at his watch.

"OK, Johnny," Chad said. "Last week, you were feeling very negative about the group. How are you feeling about us now?"

"I got nothing to say," Johnny said.

"You just said something," said William.

"Eat me," said Johnny.

At that moment a young woman of about twenty stepped through the doorway of the dank basement room.

"Is this the anonymous anonymous meeting?"

"Yes, it is, please come in," Chad said.

The girl had bleached blonde hair and enormous breasts on a child's body, but Darla recognized exhaustion and yearning on her young face as she crossed the room. She hesitated before taking the empty chair between Johnny and William.

"We go by first names here," Chad said, straightening his tie, with a welcoming smile.

"Tiffany." Her voice was soft, with a rural accent.

"Hi, Tiffany," they said in a ragged chorus. "Welcome."

She pushed her hair from her face with manicured nails and smiled shyly. "Thank you."

"We're just finishing up with Johnny," Chad told her. "But please just jump right in. So, Johnny, we started to talk last week about you getting a job."

"No job, dude. I'm gonna get on that new show, '*Dumpster*.'"

"What's that?" William asked.

"You live from a dumpster. Everything you eat, wear, and use comes out of a dumpster. Whoever lasts the longest wins."

"What do you win?" asked Tiffany.

"A million bucks. I'm gonna win. I'm gonna live in that dumpster for a year if I have to."

"Just being devil's advocate, how do you know you'll win?" said William. He had told the group that he always wanted to know details about things because if he used something in a story authentic details could make or break it.

"I don't give a shit what I eat, I don't give a shit what I wear. I don't give a shit how I smell." Johnny's eyes glowed with conviction.

"That's disgusting," Darla said.

"Darla," said Chad. "We do not make pejorative statements about members of the group."

Darla blushed. She couldn't believe Chad was calling her down.

"Do you get to pick which dumpster?" Tiffany asked. "Or do they assign you one? Because if you get to pick, you know, that could make a big difference. Some trash is better."

Johnny looked at Tiffany as if she was the first person in the group to say anything of merit. "You know what? You got a point. I'm gonna ask about that."

"If you ask me, you oughta ask for one behind a shopping mall." Tiffany's eyes met Johnny's. "There's tons of good stuff in those."

"I'm gonna. Good point, excellent point."

"Also," Tiffany added. "my mama knows a guy that picks up trash. I could introduce you. I could convince him that whenever he picks up anything really good, he should dump it in your dumpster."

"You'd do that?" Johnny moved his knee closer to Tiffany's.

"Sure, why not."

"But that's cheating!" said Darla.

"That ices it, then." Johnny said, pointedly ignoring her. "No job."

"Johnny, I'm not persuaded that you're sincere about overcoming your addiction to survival shows," said William.

"You can kiss my ass," Johnny said. "I'm gonna win 'Dumpster.' Every other contestant will be forced to say 'saronaya.'"

"I think you mean 'sayonara,'" said William in a superior voice.

"Perhaps we should move on," said Chad, with a sigh. "Darla, have you been able to resist the text messages?"

"I deleted one at the beginning of the meeting," Darla said. "And I changed my bank account numbers again. So I'm working with a clean slate, a fresh start."

"I'll alert the media," said Johnny.

"Johnny," said Chad.

Darla's phone vibrated. After a glance around the room, she opened it.

"Is it another one?" asked William.

"Yes. Should I read it?"

"Certainly. I think the group would agree that this is a good exercise for Darla," Chad said.

"OK. Here it is: 'I am the wife to businessman Rudolfo Gutierrez, who owns an oil business in Argentina. He died in a recent attack, and left with a security company the sum of seven hundred fifty million dollars meant to be used to construct an oil refinery in Asia.'"

Johnny guffawed. Tiffany chewed on her fingernail, watching Johnny.

"Seven hundred and fifty million dollars. Darla, please note; she's sending a text message to a *stranger* about seven hundred and fifty million dollars," said Chad.

Darla held up her hand. "Wait. 'I beg your assistance to help claim the funds because my husband's property has been taken over by his family who kidnapped my son and daughter the day after he died. I have nearly lost my soul because of distressing my mind.'"

"'Lost my soul because of distressing my mind?' What abysmal sentence structure," William said.

"She's from Argentina," Darla said. "Give her a break. English isn't her first language. There's more. 'I cannot come forward as I am currently being held hostage by my husband's relatives. I will give you ten percent of this money if you help. Please I beg you do not disregard this email. God bless you.'" Darla looked around the group. "I know it's crazy, but her situation touches me. She's totally alone in the world now. She's lost her children. She's lost her soul. Maybe she's being kept captive in some basement room of an Argentinean sugar cane plantation. Maybe she had access for only a few minutes to a cell phone and desperately sent out this message. I want to help her. This story is heart-breaking. Things like this really happen to people!"

"It sounds like true stories you've read or seen in movies," said William. "But if it were true, she'd just want you to save her and her children. It wouldn't be about the money."

"The thing about it is," she said, only to William now, as if it were just the two of them in the room, "there are so many people in the world who need help." She sighed, feeling a head-ache begin with a sharp stab in her left temple.

"I admire your soft-heartedness," William said. "May I copy your text message? It sounds like an engrossing sub-plot for that novel I started last night while I was in the REM dream state."

"No, she can't give it to you, William," Chad said. "That's going against everything this group stands for. You must delete it, Darla. And William, you have to throw that new novel away."

Darla cut her eyes at William, then back at Chad. Why shouldn't she be able to give William the text message? Even if she couldn't answer the message, at least she could let William copy it for his novel. Who was William hurting by writing another novel? With a defiant look at Chad, Darla thrust the phone in William's direction.

Chad lunged. His notebook tilted, splashing papers on the floor. Chad crashed into Darla's lap, his elbows slamming into her breasts at the instant she tried to lob the phone at William. Instead of catching it, William, startled, ducked, and the phone clattered across the worn gray linoleum. Through her confusion Darla saw Johnny dive for it, then collapse back into his seat with a grin.

Chad straightened Darla's skirt, and got to his feet, shaking his head. "I'm so sorry, I don't know what came over me. Darla, are you all right?" He rubbed his elbows.

"Gosh, I'm going to have some bad bruises, I think."

"I am sorry," Chad said. "As the group leader, I do apologize for my behavior."

Cradling the phone like a baby bird, Johnny let his eyes slide over at Tiffany again and again. "Heh heh, who's got it now?"

"Give me my phone." Darla cupped one hand over her sore breasts and held out her other, tears welling in her eyes. Johnny looked at the ceiling.

"Johnny," Darla said more loudly. "Give me back my phone."

"I'm helping you with your addiction," Johnny said, with a wink. "I'll just hold it until the end of the meeting."

Darla's heart beat faster. Johnny was going to force her to do something crazy. The thing to do was act as though she didn't care. If he didn't think it was bothering her, he'd put it down and she could grab it. She straightened her back, laced her fingers together in her lap, and gave an elaborate shrug. "OK, fine."

Chad had bent his glasses slightly when he landed in Darla's lap and he removed them, carefully straightened an earpiece, and slid them back on. "My apologies again. I can't imagine, Tiffany, that you would have achieved a comfort level adequate to share why you're with us, but if you have, then we will listen attentively and, of course, without judgment."

Tiffany had indeed taken two or three steps toward the door, yet Chad's words seemed to restore her confidence. "I'm here because of body image issues," she said, sitting down again.

"What do you mean?" William said, leaning forward, brandishing his pen.

"I've had a couple of plastic surgeries. Well, three. Well, four."

"How old are you?" Darla asked.

"Nineteen."

"Four plastic surgeries at nineteen? How is that possible?" Darla asked.

"My mama signed. We needed the money, and she signed."

"I didn't know you could make money getting plastic surgery. I thought you had to pay for it," Darla said. Her heart was beating faster, now, without her phone, like a nervous athlete before a match, and she was afraid she might hyperventilate. She tried to take her eyes away from Johnny's fingers mauling it, sliding all over it.

"Well, the doctors pay you if you say you'll go on TV and let them show your surgery. I reckon it's good advertising for them. So I got a pretty good deal."

"What kind of surgeries you talking about?" Johnny said. "A boob job?" He looked fixedly at her breasts.

"Yes," said Tiffany. "I went from a double A to a C. And also I wanted a bigger butt so the doctor added fat to my butt. And a nose job. And the last one I got was a labia reduction."

"A what?" Darla was so embarrassed she covered her mouth with her hand.

"They made me feel self-conscious in a bathing suit. So the doctor said I could have them reduced in size."

There was silence in the room.

"You let them show your operation on TV, didn't you?" Johnny asked. "That's where I know you from! Seriously, I saw your labia reduction surgery."

"You did?" Tiffany stared at him with anguish. "Did you think I looked fat?"

Johnny leaned forward and let the tips of his fingers brush her knee. "No."

"We got the surgery for free," Tiffany added.

"Sweet," Johnny said.

"That's completely sick," Darla said.

Tiffany looked at Darla as if she were about to cry. "I thought this was supposed to be a group where people didn't judge you."

"*I'm* not judging you," said Chad. "I blame the doctor. You were an innocent victim. A young girl, needing money. Look at the doctor's greed and flagrant self-promotion, look at the way he exploited you."

"Oh, come on!" Darla said.

"I think you got a decent deal for yourself," Johnny said. "I bet you're a helluva lot smarter than people think."

"Well, thank you," said Tiffany, with a narrow glance at Darla. "I guess *some* people think I just fell off the turnip truck.'" She nodded at Johnny and Chad, as if to show that she was grateful for their support. "But the reason I'm here, I guess, is I'm afraid I can't stop now. And I really want to do something with my life."

"I know exactly how you feel," Johnny said, leaning forward, his elbows on his knees, with an almost violent intensity. "Me, too." He clasped Darla's phone tightly under his chin. Darla was afraid he was going to crush it.

There was a shift as if the fluorescent lights had dimmed. No one spoke. Tiffany inscribed a circle in the air with the toe of her shoe.

"I think Johnny's whole attitude about this group has changed since you got here, Tiffany," said William, with a supercilious smirk at Johnny.

"Hey, I'm here because of the judge and that's it," said Johnny. "He said five sessions and this is my fifth session and I'm outta here. Vamoose. Hasta luigi."

"I believe that's 'hasta luego,'" William said, with a faint sneer.

"Shut the fuck up!" Johnny lunged, knocking over his chair, wrapping his hands around William's throat. William yelped and started gagging and the chair squealed as it scooted backwards over the linoleum, then tipped over, tumbling Johnny and William onto the floor. Darla's phone slid, twirling furiously, between the legs of her chair, and came to rest against the wall under the coffee pot

"Stop it! Stop it! Help!" Darla glanced at the phone, but in a flush of fervor, jumped up instead and tried to drag Johnny off of William, grabbing handfuls of his T-shirt and pulling with all her might.

Her eyes locked with Chad's, and that instant he kneeled and began torturously prying at Johnny's fingers one by one. Pretty soon Darla found herself lying on top of Johnny and underneath Chad, barely able to breathe.

Apparently Tiffany had run down the hall and brought back Reverend Melton, because, in her peripheral vision, Darla saw a penguin-shaped person clasping a book to his chest. Its cover featured a painting of impossibly blue skies dotted with white clouds. "What on earth is going on?"

"Oh, Reverend Melton," Chad said, untangling himself and sitting up, smoothing his hair. "My apologies. We got out of hand again today. I don't know what comes over us."

Reverend Melton drummed his fingers on the doorframe. "Folks, we've had complaints about your group every week. Dear God, now you've come to blows. I'm afraid you're going to have to find another place to meet."

"Please, just—

"I'm afraid not."

"All right, I understand." Chad took a deep breath, and stumbled to retrieve his glasses and torn posters. He picked up his notebook

Reverend Melton stood aside to let Chad leave. Johnny unlocked his hands from William's neck, and stood. He let Tiffany walk out ahead of him, touching the small of her back with the tips of his fingers.

Darla's phone was still lying under the coffee pot. Maybe she had the power to walk out of the room without it. She smoothed her skirt, and reached to help William. "William," she said, feeling reckless. "...about your poetry book..."

Reverend Melton silenced her by drumming his fingers on the doorframe again.

"Just one minute, let me get this down," William, cross-legged on the floor, shoved his dank hair behind his ear and scribbled madly on a scrap of yellow lined paper. Red imprints from Johnny's fingers splotched his neck. Darla waited, her hand out, but he didn't look up. Underneath the coffeepot, her phone began to buzz.

ANNIE'S TELEPATHIC LOVER

Tuesday afternoon Annie had an appointment with Dr. Eve Applewood, her OB/GYN, who confirmed that Annie had entered menopause. Annie curled in bed that night, taking care not to disturb her husband, who was frail from his cancer treatments. When she closed her eyes, she was visited for the first time by her telepathic lover.

In her mind's eye she could see his room. A shabby but comfortable office setting, with a worn leather couch against the wall, a native American blanket in browns and blues tossed over its back, and a small gray marble-eyed cat curled beside the arm rest. Shelves behind his chair with many books. A window beside the desk with a dream catcher hanging above the sash, and a shaft of sunlight slanting in. And she could feel his lips on her lips, on her neck, and his hands roaming her body. She could not see his face. When he entered her she quivered but her husband was tired and did not awake. There seemed to be a crackling in her brain, and she wondered if perhaps she was having a stroke or some other brain abnormality. Perhaps the sensation of having a telepathic lover was just one of a constellation of symptoms that would become more acute as time passed. After she came she felt perfectly relaxed and slept more soundly than she had since her husband's diagnosis.

A few days later she was visited again at the office, while at her computer. She was at work on a press kit and could barely finish typing the words "For Immediate Release" when she was nearly pounded through the back of her chair. No one was near her cubicle but still it was fairly embarrassing to begin to shudder like that and of course it triggered multiple hot flashes.

The following day she was in a meeting to plan an upcoming product launch and there were no less than ten people in the room discussing possible keynote speakers and their fees. She felt the soft tickle of her lover's lips on her earlobe and thought, "Oh, no, not now, please, I'm in a meeting!" but apparently he had his own agenda and she first bent over, pretending one of the legs of her chair was uneven, hoping that might explain the wobbling. Finally she said she had forgotten she had a twelve-thirty and left the meeting, running into a bathroom stall and resting her forehead against the cool metal of the door.

And then that night in the shower. And again while she was reading in bed. Annie's telepathic lover was a sex maniac. He must have sex constantly on his mind, not to mention (apparently) massive amounts of free time. Yet, in spite of the unceasing embarrassment, she never told him no.

"Who are you?" she asked, after about a week or so, but he just circled her nipple with his tongue, making her stomach turn inside-out, and did not answer.

She called Dr. Applewood. "Eve, I've been having very vivid…fantasies," she said.

"That's not unusual," Dr. Applewood assured Annie. "Many women have surges in their sex drives when they enter menopause."

"What should I do?" Annie said.

"You can't get pregnant and nobody's cheating on anybody. Enjoy them," Dr. Applewood advised.

"Easy for you to say," Annie said, wiping beads of sweat from her hairline. But she wondered if there must be someone on the other end of this. If these were simply her own fantasies, why wouldn't Annie schedule them at more convenient times?

She wandered the office, glancing in the cubicles, wondering if her lover was one of the men she worked with. None of them met her eye or seemed to have even an iota of interest in her. Finding out his identity would be very difficult. One didn't just walk up to someone and say, "Are you telepathically fucking me?" Neither did it seem to be a subject you could wend your way to during the course of any conversation Annie could think of.

She Googled two old boyfriends. Even though she hadn't heard from either of them in over twenty years, she couldn't think of anyone else it might be. One was a neurosurgeon who had recently moved nearby and while he certainly had insight into the workings of the brain, she doubted he had the free time that her telepathic lover seemed to have. The other old boyfriend, Annie learned with chagrin, was in a white collar facility serving time for tax evasion. People in jail had jobs but they probably did have more free time than the average person. She began a letter to him. "Have you been trying to contact me?" she wrote. That sounded ridiculously vague. She tried three or four other approaches and then her husband had several sleepless nights and she threw the letters away.

Usually, a few days after a treatment, her husband would be feeling well enough to go to work, and the next time that happened she took a day off and drove to the minimum security facility on the Eastern Shore where her old boyfriend was incarcerated. Soon she found herself sitting across a linoleum table from him in a visiting area.

"Have you been trying to contact me?" she said, immediately knowing, as she searched his dull, aged eyes, that he was not the one.

He scratched his head. He still had thick brown hair, only lightly sprinkled with gray. "They don't allow cell phones here," he said.

"I see." She extricated herself as soon as possible.

Initially it looked as though she would have to wait two months for the first open appointment with the brain surgeon, but when she told his scheduling nurse that she had been having hallucinations, she fit her in.

He seemed delighted to see her, and told her she didn't look a day older. She smiled and thanked him, thinking that he looked many days older. He looked exhausted, in fact. Within seconds, Annie knew that it wasn't him, either.

"So, you've been having hallucinations," he said. "That sometimes can be indicative of a tumor. We could schedule a scan."

"A scan?"

"Yes. And often if the tumor is removed, the hallucinations will go away."

Did Annie want them to go away? Suddenly she was unsure. She went outside and sat in her car, trying to decide, and her lover came to her. He caressed her face and breasts with a tenderness that brought tears to her eyes, and she went back inside and canceled the scan.

"Tell me who you are," she said to her lover the next night, when he took her from behind as she loaded her husband's stained and sour pajamas into the washing machine. "Just tell me."

But he wouldn't answer her. Her knees were pounding against the front of the machine and she couldn't even pour the detergent. "Could you come back at eleven-fifteen?" she said. "My husband needs clean pajamas. I have to get this laundry done." He did come back at eleven-fifteen, but then again at four in the morning and again at six. "Wow," she said. "This is wonderful and everything but I have to work today, and I'm going to be a wreck."

Annie's telepathic lover was much more creative and energetic than Annie's husband had ever been. As their relationship progressed it felt to Annie as though they were going through the Kama Sutra page by page. And they began talking more after making love— well, that wasn't exactly true— she pictured him cradling her in his lap the way her father had when she was a little girl— and she talked to him through her thoughts and he listened. Since he never said anything at all, he was a better listener than any man Annie had ever known.

She had never thought her husband to be a good listener. Except, sometimes, minutes or even hours after she told him about something on her mind, he surprised her by telling her what he thought she should do.

Now she never dreamed of bothering him with any of the things on her mind. She tried only to soothe and entertain him. He sat in his buttery old leather chair, seeming shrunken, his hair white and wispy, and his skin looked like wax.

She became increasingly concerned about her telepathic lover's endless supply of free time. Finally after one athletic but frankly dangerous session while she was driving home from work, she said "Do you have a regular schedule? Are we in the same time zone? You seem to be available for telepathic sex at such odd times. Not that I'm grilling you or…or trying to keep tabs on you or anything."

He of course didn't answer but she could sense him sulking. And after that she could feel him abruptly leave her. Several days went by, and he didn't come back.

Her husband became so sick he couldn't eat and had to be readmitted to the hospital and put on an IV. Annie became frantic. "Where are you?" she demanded of her lover. "Why are you sulking now? Just when I need you the most? How can you be so selfish?" She lay in her bed alone, or curled in an uncomfortable board-like chair with squeaking springs in her husband's hospital room, and couldn't believe how much she missed him. So much she thought she might die. She could literally feel herself sinking to a black and fearful place.

She apologized and begged for him to return. "I'm sorry," she said. "What business is it of mine what you do or when you do it? You're a free agent. Besides, I suppose a person could be having telepathic sex while doing any number of other productive things. Since knowing you, I've learned to multi-task that way myself. Do whatever you like, I won't ask another question. I won't even try any more to find out who you are." That night Annie was almost overcome with joy when she felt the faint crackling inside her brain signaling to her that he was back.

The night before her husband's recheck with his oncologist, Annie's telepathic lover visited her four separate times in the course of about three hours. Annie had not believed this to be humanly possible. "Are you taking something?" she asked him. She could sense he was insulted (Goodness, he was sensitive!), and covered quickly. "Of course not. Why would you need to take anything for telepathic lovemaking?"

Annie and her husband held hands in the oncologist's office.

When Dr. Divine said, "Miraculous news; I believe I can say that we are in the clear for another three months," her lover very gently kissed a half-dozen separate places on her face, his lips as cool and fleeting as snowflakes. And that night, when her husband stroked her hair and said, "Want to fool around?" Annie's telepathic lover was a perfect gentleman and did not interrupt.

FLASHLIGHT FAMILY

They were feeling celebratory; it was their oldest daughter's first night joining them at the beach and they had chosen the elegant martini bar especially with her tastes in mind. They had sat at the bar and had dirty martinis while waiting for their table, and then wine with dinner, and by the time they arrived back at their beach house, the mother had had more wine than usual and was feeling a little strange.

While her husband and two grown daughters sat on the upstairs deck to chat, drink more, and listen to the crash of the waves, the mother excused herself and went downstairs to lie down. She saw her face in the mirror briefly and was pleased to see that she looked more normal than she felt. Her chin-length graying hair kinked, as always, at the beach, and had formed a halo of frizz. Her eye sockets looked a little dark and hollow, but not frighteningly so. She had forgotten that she was supposed to watch what she drank on this medication. She lay down, listening to the pounding of the surf, to the deep bass voice of the lead singer of Crash Test

Dummies upstairs, and to her daughters' giddy laughter as they regaled her husband with college drinking tales.

She smiled, and closed her eyes, but the room spun as violently as if she were on the Tilt-a-Whirl at the amusement park. She sat up, waiting for the feeling to pass, and then lay back down again, very slowly.

She didn't know how much later it was when she awoke, but thought it was probably only a few minutes. She rose and went to the glass sliding door, looked out and was completely taken aback by the plethora of brilliant stars. She knew only a few of them—Orion's Belt, the Big Dipper, the Little Dipper, and Leo—but tonight here were so many more, swimming in a velvet sky like something painted in a passion by Van Gogh. The mother was transfixed by the splashy flamboyance of their beauty. She felt a little better and decided to try going upstairs to rejoin her family again.

She navigated the wooden outdoor steps to the upper deck, which was situated like a crow's nest, with care. Her husband placed a hand on her knee when she sat down, and she listened to the end of one of her daughter's stories about the Hillsborough Hike, which took place the night after exams were over, and students walked up and down Hillsborough Street in Raleigh drinking at every bar and then staggering to the next. She too had done things like this when in college. That had been a long time ago.

Her mind wandered and she watched a family below on the beach, all with flashlights, shining them on the sand ahead of them, walking slowly and examining what they illuminated. The mother was fascinated by the painstaking progress of the family and she wondered why they moved so slowly. What was it they were looking for there in the sand? Sand crabs? Shells? The meaning of life?

"Don't you think so, Mom?" her daughter was asking.

"I'm sorry, sweetie, what?"

Her daughter repeated her question and she answered it, thinking that the girls had both spent their first eighteen years in an intense relationship with her and now both yearned to know their father better. He was charmed by them now in a way that he had never been when they were little. The mother was not resentful or jealous; she was, rather, pleased to see her husband and daughters forming closer relationships. For one thing, it made life a bit easier for her. Solo, she had shlepped bottles and toys, made appointments for braces, made trips to the emergency room, to piano and gymnastics lessons and soccer practices. She had shopped for prom dresses and colleges and dorm bedspreads. She had loved every minute, adored her children and still did; she was just ready for the next stage of life, if she could ever figure out what that was.

The family with the flashlights had turned and were walking back toward them again, casting thin silvery cones of light onto the dark wet sand before them. The mother could barely make out the adult figures and the smaller ones, the children.

Suddenly the father raised his flashlight and seemed to point it directly at the mother. Startled, she felt transfixed by the light bedeviling her eyes. Her heart pounded hard, once, and she heard a rushing of blood in her ears. A second later the father again aimed his flashlight at the sand. Had she imagined that he'd pointed his flashlight at her?

She was seized with a desire to follow the flashlight family. Quickly, she told her husband she still didn't feel well, and went back down the rickety wooden stairs. The foot of the stairs was hidden from the upstairs porch and no one in her family would be able to see her for the first twenty yards or so as she headed down the beach. If she stayed close to the undulating sea oats, it was possible they wouldn't see her at all. Her feet sank into the cool deep sand on the pathway down to the beach and she kept her eyes on the flashlight family. She sat at the end of the path for a few moments, as the violent, pulsating stars spread above her, watching the family and hoping that when she headed across the beach that no one in her own family would notice.

Now it seemed that the father was beckoning to her, motioning with his flashlight for her to follow them. An alluring ghost effect followed his beam as it swung through the air. She rose and hurried after him, staying close to the sea oats. When she heard no one call to her from the porch above, she experienced a feeling of almost ridiculous joy at having made her getaway.

She followed the family to a curve in the beach where the beams from their flashlights seemed to multiply into several dozen, twinkling and winking in the night air like some portal to another world. The lights seemed to be waving her on to a tall house just ahead, and then they abruptly vanished. She gasped, almost running down the sand path beside the house, thinking that she had lost them, and also that she hadn't put on shoes or grabbed her purse or brushed her teeth or anything.

Now lights in the windows in the tall house began to blink on and off in a welcoming, glowworm sort of way, as if to say, "Yes, here, come here." The mother was entranced by how much all of the lights tonight reminded her of Van Gogh's "Starry Night," and wondered why that was.

When she arrived in the yard of the house, however, the windows were as dull and black as lead. She stood for several minutes, nearly overcome by a feeling of betrayal and disappointment, debating whether to go to the front door anyway. But then she understood that perhaps the blinking lights and even that entire flashlight family could have been her imagination. As she made her way back down the road to her own house, she staved off a stifling feeling of despair.

The house next to theirs had been empty all week but it had fascinated the mother. It was an old house, one-story, built in the seventies, probably. The lot was tremendously overgrown, towering with writhing, gnarled yaupon bushes with dense shiny leaves that completely blocked any view of the house from the road. Tonight the thicket throbbed with an urgent chorus of crickets and other nocturnal creatures. The house could only be seen from the ocean side. The back porch had an unusual triangular shape, and in line with the point of the porch, next to the house, stood a statue of Buddha as a young man, slim and erect, with narrow shoulders, his arms crossed over his chest. Earlier this week she had pressed her face to one of the windows, cupped her hands around her brows, and peeked inside. The house was richly decorated with heavy, centuries-old mahogany furniture, antique desk lamps with long, graceful necks, and buttery leather chairs. Thick books lay open here and there, as if a scholar of some sort had been reading earlier that morning. The mother imagined going inside and hearing sitars and the musical cascade of water in a fountain. She imagined silk floor pillows and the musky odor of burning incense. But when she tried to go a step further, to imagine the person who lived there, she could not. She longed to go inside. She had a strange feeling that if she had touched the aged brass doorknob the door would swing open as easily as a garden gate, but she had never gathered the courage to try.

Now, shivering in the heightening wind, and not ready to face her family, she managed to make it to the lower porch outside her bedroom. She sat in a creaking gray rocking chair, staring at the inviting door of the house beside her. Beyond the waving sea oats, the beach was empty. She watched for several minutes, hoping once again to see the flashlight family, but they did not reappear. As the wind continued to rise around her, she then came to hope that someone or something had come to get her, and she completely surrendered herself to this concept, She was ready to go, bare-footed as she was, and without even so much as a purse. The wind swirled and whistled as it had in the opening scenes of the Wizard of Oz, and the mother felt it might be possible for the wind to lift her directly into the air the way it had Dorothy's house. "I want to fly," she said, but though the wind continued to buffet her rocking chair, she was never lifted into the air, or whisked away, and she came to understand that this, too, was merely her imagination.

Everyone was still on the outside back porch, and she went to the front of her own house and slitted the door open. Above her head the electrical wires were crackling and houses that hadn't been lit up all week blazed with light. A vehicle, half a block away, blinded her with dozens of orange beams. A power truck, she realized. Perhaps the high winds had caused some problem. If she walked out there, into the vortex of wind and blazing lights, she imagined—knowing, now, truly, that it was only her imagination—that she might be transported to somewhere new.

With some effort, she shut the door and returned to her bedroom to lie down. In a few minutes, she would smooth her hair and put on more lipstick and go upstairs to listen to her children's stories. Tomorrow, she would try the doorknob at the house next door.

Special Thanks

Some of these stories were written or revised while I was in the Queens University MFA program, and I'd like to thank my teachers and fellow students for their guidance. In particular, Louise Rockwell's generosity and support have meant so much to me. My friend Susie Lawson read and commented on these stories and I am grateful for her feedback. I especially want to thank Suzanne Baldwin Leitner for her encouragement and wise insight on final drafts and in ordering the stories.

I appreciate Rick Bray of Skyride taking the time to answer my questions about skydiving for "Groundrush."

Many thanks to Scott Douglass for choosing my work for the honor of publication and for his guidance through the process.

For her fabulous cover art, I must recognize Kelsey Kline, and for her unflagging moral support, Caitlin Kline.

Most of all, I thank my dear and steadfast husband Jeff.